What the critics are saying...

"Jory Strong's Lyric's Cop is deliciously sexy." ~ *Cynthia, A Romance Review*

"Jory Strong's writing ability had me laughing out loud at times, and Lyric is a great character. She's strong and feisty, and she is wildly attracted to Kieran. Kieran is a strong alpha male, who is strongly attracted to Lyric and determined to keep her safe despite herself... Who knew that being a pet detective could be interesting and dangerous?" ~ *Julia, The Romance Studio*

"Crime Tells 1: Lyric's Cop has it ALL! Strong characters, witty dialogue, blazing sex scenes, and a great plot combine to make this a page turner that will stay in your reread files for a long time." ~ *Trang Noire, Just Erotic Romance Reviews*

"A romance with just as much plot as action, *Crime Tells 1: Lyric's Cop* was more than able to pull me in and keep me reading till the end. The plot starts out with a simple dog napping and grows to include deeply sinister plans...The wild sensations of give and pull between these two characters kept me hot and bothered throughout the book. I greatly enjoyed seeing the growth from wild sex to deeper feelings in this somewhat tumultuous relationship. *Crime Tells 1: Lyric's Cop* is one of the few books that I would happily read again." ~ *Francesca Hayne , Just Erotic Romance Reviews*

JORY STRONG

Crime Tells

Lyric's COP

ELLORA'S CAVE
ROMANTICA PUBLISHING

An Ellora's Cave Romantica Publication

www.ellorascave.com

Lyric's Cop

ISBN # 141995251X
ALL RIGHTS RESERVED.
Lyric's Cop Copyright© 2005 Jory Strong
Edited by: Sue-Ellen Gower
Cover art by: Syneca

Electronic book Publication: March, 2005
Trade paperback Publication: September, 2005

Excerpt from *Cady's Cowboy* Copyright ©Jory Strong 2005

Warning:

The following material contains graphic sexual content meant for mature readers. *Lyric's Cop* has been rated *E-rotic* by a minimum of three independent reviewers.

Ellora's Cave Publishing offers three levels of Romantica™ reading entertainment: S (S-ensuous), E (E-rotic), and X (X-treme).

S-ensuous love scenes are explicit and leave nothing to the imagination.

E-rotic love scenes are explicit, leave nothing to the imagination, and are high in volume per the overall word count. In addition, some E-rated titles might contain fantasy material that some readers find objectionable, such as bondage, submission, same sex encounters, forced seductions, etc. E-rated titles are the most graphic titles we carry; it is common, for instance, for an author to use words such as "fucking", "cock", "pussy", etc., within their work of literature.

X-treme titles differ from E-rated titles only in plot premise and storyline execution. Unlike E-rated titles, stories designated with the letter X tend to contain controversial subject matter not for the faint of heart.

Also by Jory Strong:

Lyric's Cop
Crime Tells

Trademarks Acknowledgement

The author acknowledges the trademarked status and trademark owners of the following wordmarks mentioned in this work of fiction:

Cadillac: General Motors Corporation

Corvette: General Motors Corporation

Ford: Ford Motor Company

Harley: Harley-Davidson Motor Company

Jeep: DaimlerChrysler

Liar's Dice: MTGR Corporation DBA Murphy-Goode Estate Winery

Technicolor: Technicolor Motion Picture Corporation

White Shoulders: Evyan Perfumes, Inc.

Prologue

The man couldn't believe his luck. He'd stopped at a local convenience store for a pack of cigarettes and heard a kid telling his friend about an old lady and her three wiener dogs — and here she was.

"Bingo. Ain't this gonna be a piece of cake." He eased his black van over to the curb, retrieving a cigarette from the pack in his shirt pocket as he got out. "Come on, Granny. I ain't got all day." He moved to the side of the van, opening the sliding door and pretended to rummage around.

Unaware, the woman continued toward him, the dachshunds — two reds and a black — darting back and forth on either side of her as they investigated the smells along the sidewalk and bordering fence. Every few steps she paused to give the dogs a little extra time for an interesting spot.

"Hurry it, Granny. You're starting to piss me off."

As the woman drew near to the van, the dogs noticed the beefy man and slid closer to their owner. The largest of the three growled deep in his throat.

"Now, now, babies. It's just someone cleaning out their van." The old woman stopped and reached down to give the dogs a reassuring pat.

The man stood up, but kept his back to the woman and her dogs. He looked up and down the street. Not a soul in sight. Out of the corner of his eye he saw the old lady straighten up and begin walking. In another minute she would be just where he wanted her. He tensed, ready to get this over with so he could get paid. He had a beer and a whore waiting for him down at Turbo's.

As the woman and her dogs walked past the open door of the van, the man turned and grabbed the leashes. The dogs erupted into furious barking as the woman jerked backward in surprise.

The old lady's grip was surprisingly strong. He hadn't counted on that. "Let go, Granny," he growled as he tried to twist the leashes out of her grip.

Teeth sunk into his ankle. He shook the dog off. Panic set in. This wasn't going down smoothly. Any minute now someone could drive down the street and see what was happening. Then he'd be back in the joint. Pissed, he flung a giant arm out and slammed the old lady into the fence. She hit with enough force to stop her struggles. He yanked the leashes out of her hand and used them to jerk the dogs into his van.

Within seconds he had the sliding door shut and was sitting in the driver's seat. Any minute he expected to hear sirens blaring. "Fuck, who would have thought the old lady would struggle?" His beefy face was flushed and sweat began to trickle past his eyebrows.

The elderly woman could hear her dogs barking furiously as the van pulled away from the curb. Her head and arms hurt, she felt dizzy and couldn't even attempt to get up. Tears of pain and anguish rolled down her face as the van sped around a corner and disappeared.

Chapter One

Lyric Montgomery looked at the small blurb in the newspaper and knew that she couldn't ignore it. She just had a feeling... She half-smiled, half-grimaced, knowing how that sounded to most people, but what the hell—it was true. And she came by it naturally—an inheritance from the Maguire side of the family.

Even Bulldog had a respect for Grandma Maguire's premonitions. Lyric grinned—of course, Bulldog had a healthy respect for the laws of chance. Until he'd semi-retired, Bulldog Montgomery was one of the most sought-after detectives in the gambling business. Casinos all over the country hired him when they thought they were being ripped-off, either by gamblers or their own employees.

He still worked those cases occasionally, but for the most part, he'd gotten tired of living out of a suitcase—even though the suitcase was parked in exclusive hotel rooms, complete with complimentary meals. These days he wanted to spend more time with his grandchildren. So he'd started Crime Tells—*Tell* being a gambling term for the clues or hints that players or dealers unknowingly give about the cards they control.

Now Bulldog took on a wide variety of cases in Northern California, anything that grabbed his interest or seemed like something his grandchildren would enjoy working on. Besides Lyric and her sisters, Cady and Erin, Crime Tells also employed their cousins, Shane, Braden and Cole.

Some days Lyric felt like pinching herself to make sure she wasn't dreaming. Not only did she get to work with her sisters and occasionally her cousins, but her grandfather encouraged them all to pursue their own interests. Cady and Erin were both professional pet photographers while Lyric considered herself a pet detective.

That they'd end up in animal-related professions was almost a given. Their father was a distinguished biologist working to preserve habitat around the world and their mother was an extraordinary nature photographer.

Bulldog loved to laugh and say that all of his grandkids had taken to the detective business like dogs to a bone. Lyric was no exception.

She looked down at the blurb again. It was little more than a by-the-way inclusion in the newspaper. But it sent a tingling combination of dread and anticipation right through her.

A seventy-nine-year-old woman walking her three dachshunds in the Willow Glen area was accosted and her dogs stolen. The woman, Anna Simmons, was taken to the hospital overnight for observation. Police continue looking for information or eyewitnesses to the crime. The suspect is a heavyset man driving a black van. Anyone with knowledge of this individual should come forward by contacting the police department directly or calling the anonymous tip line.

Lyric reached for the telephone book and went right to the white pages. There were three A. Simmons listed, but only one in the Willow Glen area. She took a deep breath and dialed. This was the first cold call she'd ever made. Until now, all of the cases not directly connected to Crime Tells had come from veterinarians, humane societies, rescue groups and word of mouth referrals.

Anna Simmons answered the phone and sent a shiver right down Lyric's spine when Lyric didn't even get past her own name before the obviously elderly lady said, "Will you help me find my dogs?"

"You know who I am?"

"There was an article about you in the newspaper a couple of months ago. I had a feeling about it when I read it. So I clipped it out. It's been in my purse for months." There was a shaky indrawn breath. "I never thought I'd need your services myself. Can you find my dogs?" Anna's voice was threaded with pain and hope. It begged for someone to offer comfort and assurance—to tell her that the dogs would be found and safely returned.

Lyric's heart ached. Besides telling someone that their pet's body had been recovered, this was the worst part of what she did—trying to walk a tightrope between hope and reality. "I don't know. I'll need more information."

"Then you'll help?" Anna's voice cracked mid-sentence.

"Yes, I want to come by and talk with you as soon as possible." Lyric was worried. Animal thefts didn't go down like this—well, unless maybe there was a custody dispute. That didn't seem to be the case here.

"Can you come right now?"

"Are you up to it?"

"Yes, I have a terrible feeling that if I don't act quickly, I'll never get them back."

"I'll head over." Lyric stopped just long enough to send e-mail to her sisters and to Bulldog to inform them that she was off on a case.

A Harley was parked in front of Anna Simmons' house. Lyric grinned when she saw it. She had a Harley at home, the sole occupant of her garage. And like her bike, this one was someone's prized possession. The black paint and chrome sparkled like it had just rolled off the assembly line. Definitely not an old lady's wheels.

Tearing herself away from the polished beauty, Lyric hustled up the long walk to Anna's house and knocked. The door opened and she found herself confronted by a sight even more tantalizing than the Harley—the Harley's owner.

He was drop-dead, bad-boy gorgeous. Black hair, blue eyes, a body worth fantasizing over and a five o'clock shadow that he probably had within hours of shaving. In a word—Black Irish and a damned fine specimen.

He was also blocking the doorway, frowning in a way that let her know he was no stranger to the use of intimidation. Then again, intimidation had never worked very well on Lyric, and coming from a guy who looked like this one, it only turned her on. She stepped closer, crowding into his personal space. "I'm here to see Anna Simmons."

Tall-dark-and-trying-to-be-scary opened his mouth to say something but before he had a chance to speak, a woman's voice said, "Please let her in, Kieran."

Kieran shot Lyric a warning glance then stepped out of the way. Anna Simmons moved into view. She was just about what Lyric had expected—grandmotherly and haggard from both the brush with violence and the theft of her dogs.

"Lyric, this is my grandson, Kieran Burke. Kieran, this is the detective I was telling you about, Lyric Montgomery. Don't let Kieran put you off, Lyric. He's very upset by what's happened."

Right. Lyric looked at Kieran. The tension in his body made it plain that the assault on his grandmother and the theft of her dogs wasn't the only thing he was upset about. He was pissed that she was there. Then again—heat rushed over Lyric's nipples as her gaze drifted to the erection pushing against the front of his jeans—parts of him weren't upset.

Anna ushered them into the living room. The house was small and cozy, the furnishings tasteful but not luxurious. The walls were covered with family pictures, including one of a much younger and definitely smiling Kieran. Lyric couldn't resist comparing it to the real thing. The more mature version had lived up to his earlier potential, at least when it came to looks.

Lyric picked a chair and sat down. Kieran positioned himself on the couch, right across from her.

"Can I get you a cup of coffee or something to drink?" Anna asked.

Lyric shook her head. "No, thanks."

Kieran didn't take his eyes off Lyric as he said, "I'd like a cup of coffee."

A look of uncertainty danced across Anna's face, but short of rescinding the offer or demanding her grandson accompany her, she was stuck. Lyric thought they were both relieved when Kieran got out of his seat and followed his grandmother into the kitchen.

Son of a bitch. Could it get any worse? If this didn't complicate his life in painful ways, Kieran didn't know what would. Three seconds and he had a hard-on that would double as a nightstick. Goddamn—Braden Maguire's cousin, Bulldog Montgomery's granddaughter.

Oh yeah, he remembered the stories Braden used to tell about his cousin, Lyric—the lawbreaker. Not that Braden didn't have a little trouble staying in the lines himself. That was one of the reasons he hadn't stayed a cop very long before quitting and going to work for Bulldog, but Braden had been a cop long enough to share plenty of beers down at Henry's. Goddamn, Braden had even talked about setting Kieran up with Lyric. If he'd had any idea... Fuck.

Yeah, that was the problem. He'd never been so turned on so fast. Christ, he wanted to tunnel his fingers through her thick black curls, fall into the blue sea of her eyes and shove his cock in and out of her. Shit! He didn't need this right now. It'd be hard to stay focused, to keep a cool head if Lyric was working this case.

Kieran didn't bother shutting the door behind him. He wanted Lyric to overhear what he had to say and back out of the case on her own. He already knew going in how stubborn his grandmother could be. And there wasn't a chance in hell that he'd get her to change her mind about hiring Lyric.

"Grandma, I told you I'd take care of this. You don't need to waste your money on an outside detective."

"It's not a waste of money, Kieran." Anna's voice was surprisingly strong and determined. "Lyric is a pet detective. This is her specialty. She tracks down lost pets for a living. I read about her in the newspaper."

"Yeah, and the other day when I was in the grocery store I read about aliens taking over the White House. That doesn't mean I believe it!"

"Kieran, you spend too much of your time around criminals. I'm not talking about that kind of newspaper and you know it!" Anna actually managed a laugh. "I've got the article about her right here in my purse."

"Ok, Grandma. You win. Look, I've already called in a few favors. We take care of our own, so the case will get some attention. Your report won't end up sitting in a pile of papers on someone's desk. Save your money. Let the police handle it. I'll even ask the captain for some time off so I can investigate it personally."

Anna chuckled. "Kieran, if you want to take some time off and help Lyric, I'm sure she would appreciate that. But I had a premonition that she's the one who can find the dogs."

"Grandma..."

"Calm down and don't roll your eyes. There's no need to get yourself worked up. I know you don't understand about my 'feels' but I've relied on them all my life, and they haven't failed me yet. The article about Lyric is a perfect example of what I mean. I read it a couple of months ago and clipped it out of the newspaper. Now I need it. Why don't you read it? I think you'll feel better after you know a little bit more about Lyric."

"Please, Grandma, let the police handle it. Let me handle it."

"Thank you for offering, Kieran. I'm lucky to have a grandson like you. Now here's your coffee. I want you to behave yourself when we go back in there."

Lyric managed to plaster on a no-I'm-not-thinking-of-kicking-you-in-the-nuts smile and waited for them to take their seats. "Okay then," she said, focusing on Anna and making a point of ignoring Kieran. "I'd like you to tell me what happened. As you go, I'm going to ask you some questions."

Anna nodded. "Yesterday morning I was walking my dachshunds on Marques Avenue. We were taking our time—my three love to keep their noses to the ground and investigate every interesting smell. I noticed a man standing near a black van. His back was turned to us and it looked like he was cleaning out the van. I'm afraid that I didn't really pay any attention to him. But Max must have known that something wasn't right because he growled at the man—which isn't like Max at all." Anna's composure slipped and tears started trailing down her cheeks. "I should have known something was wrong. If I'd just paid attention to what Max was trying to tell me…"

Kieran glowered at Lyric as he moved over to slip an arm around his grandmother's shoulders. Lyric scowled back before leaning forward and gently squeezing Anna's hand. "Please, don't upset yourself with those kinds of thoughts. There's no way you could have guessed what the man was up to. No one could have. I've never heard of a theft like this one. It was totally unpredictable."

Anna struggled with her emotions for a moment longer, then took a deep breath and continued. "As I passed by him, he turned and grabbed the leashes. It happened so quickly that I didn't even have a chance to scream. When I wouldn't let go, he shoved me into a fence and I hit my head. I vaguely remember him putting my dogs in the van and driving away. The next thing I remember is that a woman with a small child was standing over me. She must have called 911 because the paramedics and the police got there a few minutes later and I was taken to the hospital."

"Did the woman see anything?"

"I don't know. I didn't even have a chance to thank her for helping me. There was so much confusion when the ambulance arrived...all those people rushing around."

Lyric looked at Kieran. She could pretend that she hadn't overheard the conversation in the kitchen or she could just ask him the question that needed to be asked. "I assume the police questioned the woman who called 911. Do you know whether or not she saw anything?"

"She didn't," he growled.

Lyric turned her attention back to Anna. "What time were you attacked?"

"Around ten-thirty, I think. We do the same walk every day. It takes an hour and a half. Usually we start at seven, right after breakfast. Only yesterday I was running behind. So we left later than normal."

Lyric's eyebrows drew together. So was the man after Anna's dogs specifically? Or was it a random act—just a case of being in the wrong place at the wrong time? "The newspaper said the man was heavy-set. Can you remember any identifying features?"

Anna closed her eyes briefly. "No."

"What about hair and eye color?"

"Brown hair. Green eyes—or blue." She sighed, frustrated. "I'm not sure about the color of his eyes."

"What about height and weight?"

Anna looked over at her grandson. "He was just a little shorter than Kieran, maybe a couple of inches, but a lot heavier."

"Would you recognize him again?"

Anna hesitated. "I think so."

"Have the police already talked to you about going down to the station and looking through their mug shots?"

"Yes. The officer who visited me in the hospital told me to come down when I'm able to."

"Good. I'd like to go with you. Give me a call when you're ready and I'll drive you."

"I'd like to go tomorrow."

"I don't think so, Grandma. You're in no condition to go down there and sit. I'll have an artist come out and work up a sketch. Then I can go through the pictures and narrow it down for you."

Anna nodded and Lyric decided that it was the perfect opportunity to get things out on the table. "You're a cop?"

"Yeah. Vice."

Lyric almost smiled at that. Oh yeah, she could see how down and dirty would appeal to him. He was probably great at what he did. "I want a copy of the artist's sketch. And if you get a hit on the picture, I want to know the particulars."

Kieran's eyes narrowed. "We'll see."

Lyric met his eyes and sent a silent challenge before shifting her focus back to Anna. "Can you remember anything else about the man or the van he was driving?"

"Now that I think about it, it was an older Ford van."

"What about the man? Do you remember anything else?"

Anna was silent. "He was smoking. When I first noticed him, he had a cigarette in his hand."

"Is there any reason for someone to think that the dogs are valuable?"

Anna gave a weak smile. "They're priceless to me. But no, they aren't valuable. They aren't show dogs or anything like that, they're just pets."

"Have you noticed any strangers hanging around the neighborhood lately?"

"No. We've got a neighborhood watch here. I haven't noticed anyone and I'm pretty friendly with most of my neighbors. They would have told me if anyone was snooping around."

Lyric nodded. Her gut told her that the man who'd taken the dogs didn't know where Anna lived. If he'd known, he would have opted for an easier way to steal them.

"Where did you get the dogs?"

"I got all three of them from Caroline, she's involved in rescue work."

"Do you have any background on them?"

"Yes. All three came from the same home. The woman who owned them was trying to escape an abusive situation. She turned them over to rescue and fled to Canada with her two small children."

"And that was the end of any contact with her?"

Anna gave her grandson a wary look. "No. A couple of months after I adopted the dogs, Caroline called to tell me that the woman was coming back to her husband and wanted the dogs returned. When Caroline told the husband that they couldn't have the dogs back, he was quite abusive over the phone, then he showed up at her house. Caroline called to let me know there might be a problem, just in case I ran into the couple. She knew that I take the dogs everywhere with me."

"Grandma, why didn't you tell me all this?"

"There wasn't anything to worry about. The people didn't know who had the dogs or where they were. Besides, that was almost eight months ago."

"I want Caroline's address and phone number," Kieran said.

Anna stood and Lyric said, "I'll need photographs of the dogs, and complete descriptions, too."

"Let me get that for you."

Kieran waited until his grandmother left the room before leaning forward and saying, "There isn't going to be any bullshit here. One wrong move and…"

Anna returned and set the pictures on the table before opening her address book and providing Caroline's information. Lyric took it down then moved to the top picture. Anna pointed to a red dog, identifying her as Heidi. The second red female was Gretchen. The black male, Max.

Lyric looked through the remaining pictures, placing several photographs to the side. When she got to the last one, she said, "I'd like to take these. I'll give them back to you when I'm finished with them."

"There's no hurry. Keep them as long as you need to."

"Okay, just a few more questions and we'll be done. Are the dogs spayed and neutered?"

"Oh yes. In fact, I picked them up from the veterinarian. I saw them the day after they got to Caroline's home. I signed an adoption contract there. Then she took them to the vet for their surgeries. I paid the vet for the medical work and brought them home."

"Are they tattooed or microchipped?"

"Microchipped. I'll have to dig up their veterinary papers to find out what their numbers are. Do you need that right now?" Anna was beginning to look worn down.

"No. I've got enough information to start with." Lyric pulled out two business cards. Laying the first one down on the table, she said, "This is my personal card." She put the second one down. "But if it's urgent and you can't get me, I also work for my grandfather's agency. The number on this card will always reach a live person. So if I can't be found, then my sisters or my cousins or even my grandfather will help you."

Tears formed at the corners of Anna's eyes. "You'll find my dogs. I know you will."

Lyric reached over and squeezed Anna's hands before standing. "I'll do everything I can...including getting started right now."

Kieran stood, too. "You stay there, Grandma. I'll see Lyric out."

He waited until they got to the front door before crowding into Lyric's space. "I'm going to get my grandmother settled, then you and I are going to have a discussion about how this case is going to play out."

Lyric laughed. What else could she do? His macho, I'm-in-control attitude tempted her like fire tempted a pyromaniac.

Chapter Two

Still, Lyric did not stick around for the lecture. She had a feeling that she was going to have to move fast if she expected to get the jump on Kieran. She was calling Caroline of dachshund rescue even as she drove away from Anna's house.

Caroline answered on the second ring and laughed as soon as Lyric mentioned that she'd gotten the number from Anna. "She's certainly been one of my best adopters. Everywhere she goes people fall in love with her dogs. What can I do for you?"

"I'm hoping you can give me some additional information about the people who owned Anna's dogs before she got them. Yesterday they were stolen from her while she was walking them. Anna's hired me to help get them back."

"My God! Is Anna all right?"

"She spent the night in the hospital for observation. But I think the worst part is the theft of her dogs."

"Oh my. This is horrible. I've never had anything like this happen to one of my rescue dogs."

"What can you tell me about the former owners?"

"It was a bad situation. Let me get the adoption contract out. I had trouble with the original owners and so I documented everything I could." There was the sound of rattling papers. "Okay. I got the dogs from Linda Surbeck about a year ago. She called me on a Monday morning just as I was getting ready to run errands. I remember it because she sounded terrified. When I tried to get her to meet me with the dogs later in the day she panicked. It took me five minutes to calm her down. Finally I agreed to see her right away."

"What did she look like?"

"She was young, early twenties. She had two small children in the car but she didn't take them out. I can't tell you how old they were, only that both were still in car seats. She was just a little taller than I am, so maybe five-four. Her face was caked with makeup, but it didn't hide the damage. She'd been severely beaten."

"Did she give you any details about her situation?"

"No, and I didn't press. She was very nervous. Every few minutes she'd look over her shoulder. It made me pretty anxious myself."

"What color hair did she have?"

"Dyed blonde, with very dark roots. It hung down past her shoulders."

"Would you recognize her again?"

There was a pause. "I'm not sure I would. I tried not to look at her face. She was so nervous, I didn't want to scare her off."

"Was anyone with her besides the kids?"

"No. There were bags in the car and she told me that she was on her way to Canada. I remember thinking that she was running from her husband or a boyfriend."

"Anna told me that a couple of months later Linda wanted her dogs back."

On the other end of the line, Caroline sighed. "Yes, two months later I got a call from her husband. His name was Gene. He told me that Linda wanted her dogs back."

"What did you do?"

"I told him that the dogs were in a good home and that legally I couldn't get them back."

"How did he take it?"

"Not very well, he started cursing and threatening me. The next day I opened my door and found this big beefy man standing there."

Lyric's pulse jumped. The man who'd attacked Anna was a large beefy guy. "That probably got your heart racing."

Caroline laughed. "And them some. It was terrifying. Luckily a friend happened to be over at the time."

"What happened?"

"Linda's husband demanded that I tell him where the dogs were. I lied and told him they were with a woman in Santa Clara, but I didn't remember her name or address."

"Did he believe you?"

"I don't know whether he did or not. But with my friend here, he couldn't coerce me into telling him anything. I told him I would look for the new owner's phone number and see if she wanted to give the dogs back—or that I would give his number to her so that he could ask her himself if she chose to call him."

"How did Surbeck react when you told him that?"

"He seemed to calm down. It may sound cruel to say this, but he didn't strike me as particularly intelligent. I don't think he had any idea of the records we keep in rescue. I've got a logbook of every phone call that's ever come in. And of course, the dogs all go out on adoption contracts. So we have adopter work and home phone numbers, addresses, and driver license numbers."

"Was his wife with him the day he came by?"

"No. Later I got to thinking that maybe he was trying to get the dogs back in order to pressure her into coming back to him."

"What makes you say that?"

"I guess because I've never heard from her. When she brought me the dogs I got the feeling that she really cared about them. If she was back in town I think she would call, even if it was just to find out how they are."

"Did you notice what kind of car he was driving?"

"No. I was so rattled that all I could think about was getting rid of him. Afterward I kicked myself for not noticing his car and writing down his license plate number."

"Did you call the police?"

There was a pause on the other end of the line. "No. I wanted to, but I was afraid they would need to come to the house for a statement."

She didn't need to say anything more. Lyric had met a large number of animal rescue people. The one thing they all had in common was a fear of having the authorities come to their houses. Most of them had well over the legal number of animals at any given point in time. "Would you recognize him again?"

"Definitely." Caroline's voice was sure and firm.

"Did you get a phone number or address from Gene Surbeck or his wife?"

"I didn't get an address, but I did get a phone number from him."

Lyric took down the number. "Have you heard from Surbeck since that visit?"

"No. I called him back the next day, more to avoid having him show up at my door again, than to keep my promise. Thankfully he wasn't there, so I left a message on his answering machine. I told him that I couldn't find the adopter's phone number."

"And you didn't notice anyone suspicious hanging around your neighborhood or following you?"

"No. And believe me, I looked over my shoulder for weeks. But there was never anything strange or unnerving."

"Anything else you can think of?"

There was a pause. "It may be nothing, but last week I got three calls from people who had lost their dachshunds. I remember thinking it was strange to have so many dogs lost in such a short time. Usually I only get a couple of lost dog calls a year."

A tingling sensation raced along Lyric's spine—this was what she'd suspected, what she'd dreaded when she read the blurb in the newspaper and felt the compulsion to call—that Anna's dogs weren't an isolated incident. "Do you still have their names and phone numbers?"

"Hold on a second. Let me get my logbook." There was the sound of a desk drawer being opened. "Here they are. The first one was a spayed red female. The owner left her in the yard just long enough to run to the grocery store. When he came back the dog was gone." Caroline read off the owner's name and phone number. "It was a miniature."

"The next was a black unspayed female. She was also a miniature. Same thing, the owner left her in the yard for the day. When she got back the gate was open. She blamed it on the meter reader."

"Now the last one was day before yesterday. A black male. Unneutered, also a miniature."

"What were the circumstances of his disappearance?"

"Same thing, I'm afraid. It's a very depressing situation. The owners went away overnight and left the dog with 'plenty of food' in the backyard. They left in the morning and didn't check on him again until the next evening."

"Dachshunds can be real diggers, any signs of digging in any of these cases?"

"No. I asked. And you're right, they can be diggers." Caroline paused. "Do you think the disappearances are related?"

"Yes. That's six dogs in a little over a week."

"Do you think someone is taking them for resale?" She sounded as distressed as Lyric felt.

"Yes. I think a call has gone out from a puppy-mill operation or research organization saying that they need a certain number of this breed by a certain date."

"Dear God, that's horrible! It makes me sick to think of animals crowded into pens and kept pregnant so that their puppies can be sold with no thought at all about what kinds of homes they'll end up in, or what quality of life they'll have. And the alternative, research… I can't stand thinking about it."

"Let me give you my phone numbers. If you hear about any other dogs disappearing, please call me right away, and it's okay to leave information with my sisters if you get them."

"I certainly will."

Lyric started the Jeep and drove to a pay phone, curious to find out if Gene Surbeck was still around, but not wanting to chance that he might be using a cell and could end up with her number. An answering machine picked up. She could hear a kid crying in the background while a man's voice told her to leave a message. She passed on the suggestion and hung up.

An answering machine meant it was a landline. Her PDA made it easy to connect to the web and use a reverse directory to find a corresponding address, then plug the address into a map program.

Surbeck was on Keeble Avenue, not close enough to Anna's neighborhood to make it likely that he'd stumbled across Anna walking her dogs. But not far enough away to rule it out completely. Lyric grimaced, wondering if Kieran was already on his way to Keeble.

She checked her notes and called the owners of the other three missing dogs. Voice mail recorded a message for two of them, a man answered the third.

"Have you found her?" he asked as soon as Lyric identified herself. There was such hope in his voice that her heart squeezed in response.

"No, I'm sorry. I'm working on another case involving miniature dachshunds. I was hoping that I could ask you some questions. Caroline from dachshund rescue gave me your name and number."

"Oh." He sounded defeated and heartsick. "It's been over a week now. Every day that passes makes it less likely she'll come back to me."

Lyric wanted to offer him hope to balance the harsh truth, but knew the best thing she could do was say, "If you don't mind telling me what happened then I'll keep an eye out for your dog as well."

"Anything, anything I can do to get Emily back. What do you need to know?"

"Caroline told me that your dog disappeared while you were at the grocery store. Do you remember how long you were gone?"

"Yes. I was only gone for about forty minutes. I don't usually leave Emily in the yard, but it was such a beautiful day, and she was having so much fun playing in the grass that I just couldn't bring myself to make her come inside. God, I wish I'd done it, then she'd still be here." He sounded close to tears.

"Did she have a collar and tags on?"

"Oh yes. She's never without identification. I always worry that in an earthquake she might get out and get lost."

"Good for you. Ninety-five percent of pets found with tags do get home." She spared him the opposite fact— ninety-five percent of lost pets found without a tag don't get home. "Mr. Merriman..."

"Please, call me John."

"John, do you have any idea how Emily got out of your yard?"

"No. I've looked over every inch of my fencing. I couldn't find a single spot where I thought she could get out."

"Would it be easy for someone to see her if they were driving or walking by your house?"

"I don't think so."

"Does she know the neighborhood? Do you walk her?"

"I walk her two or three times a day."

"Do you walk at about the same time each day?"

"Yes, I walk her first thing in the morning, somewhere around nine. Then sometimes I walk her at around two-thirty, just when the school kids are getting out. She loves kids and I like for her to spend time with them. Then I walk her in the early evening, maybe at around six."

"Is Emily microchipped?"

"No. The vet told me about it, but I just never thought she'd get away from me..."

"I understand. How old is Emily?"

"She just turned four. I've had her since she was a puppy." He paused. "My wife passed away four years ago. I lost her to cancer. It was pretty lonely here in the house. My kids are all out of state, so I don't get to see them or the grandkids very much. A friend suggested that I get a dog, he even loaned me his dog for a weekend. It was a little dachshund and I got hooked on the breed."

"Caroline said that the dog is a red female. Does she have any distinguishing marks on her?"

"As a matter of fact, she does. She's got a nick on her right ear. It's not very big, but you'd notice it if you were looking for it." He laughed. "She's a feisty little dog. As a pup I took her back east to visit my son. Brian has a Blue and Gold macaw. That bird took one look at Emily and climbed down off of its stand to get a better view. Emily charged right up to it and the bird took a bite out of her ear. I felt so terrible! It never even occurred to me that a bird would do that! Anyway, we rushed her to the vet, who said it would heal just fine and that it didn't make sense to sew it back together." He laughed again. "Now Emily avoids any birds that are bigger than she is."

Lyric grinned. Even though she hadn't met John, she liked him. "Would it be possible for me to come by and get a picture of Emily?"

"Anytime. I'm here most days. I've put up reward posters and called in a lost dog ad to the local newspaper. So for the last week I've been trying to stick pretty close to the phone." There was a moment's hesitation. "I've offered a five hundred dollar reward, but I could come up with more. Do you think it's enough?"

"It's more than enough. Most of the time the person who finds a lost animal doesn't even insist on the reward. For the most part they care about animals or have been in the same situation themselves and are glad to help out."

"That's good to hear. I've been worried that it wasn't enough. I would have expected a call by now."

"What day did Emily disappear?"

"Last Monday. It must have happened somewhere between ten and eleven in the morning."

"Did you notice any suspicious people or unfamiliar cars in the neighborhood around the time she disappeared?"

"There was no one suspicious." John sounded very definite. "I live on a very quiet street. I'm sure I didn't see any strangers hanging around."

"What about unfamiliar cars?"

There was silence as John thought about the question. "Now that you mention it, I did see a red Corvette in the neighborhood. I noticed it a couple of times. I've always dreamed of owning a car like that, otherwise I probably wouldn't have even seen it."

"Did you notice a driver?"

"No. I'm afraid I only had eyes for the car." John was quiet for a moment. In a very somber voice he asked, "Do you think Emily was taken from my yard?" Pain washed down the phone line and Lyric felt drenched in it.

She hesitated. "It's possible. Last week three dachshunds disappeared. Yesterday my client was knocked down while she was walking her three dogs and the dogs were stolen. We don't know for certain that Emily's disappearance has anything to do with my client's dogs. But I'll do what I can to look for her."

"Thank you."

"If it's all right with you, I'll come by tomorrow for the picture."

"I'll be here all day."

Lyric closed her cell phone, not surprised to see the Harley pull up behind her. Just watching Kieran as he swung off the bike and removed his helmet was enough to have her body tightening with anticipation. She got out of the Jeep so he wouldn't have the advantage of hovering over her.

"You talked to Caroline," he said, stopping in her personal space, surrounding her with his body heat and masculine scent.

"Yeah. I'm sure you talked to her, too."

"Caroline told you about Surbeck and you came up with an address for him, so that's where you're heading, right?"

Lyric shrugged. "Maybe."

Goddamn, did she have any idea what her challenging attitude did to him? His eyes narrowed. Hell yeah, from the hot, knowing little look in her eyes, she'd probably gotten a good view of the front of his jeans. *Yeah, baby, get a good look so you know what's coming your way.*

"Anna wants us to work together on this." The partial truth rolled off Kieran's tongue and tasted like vinegar.

A more accurate representation of what happened after Lyric left his grandmother's house was that *he'd* received a lecture on *his* behavior and a plea that he not make things difficult for Lyric. If that wasn't a pisser he didn't know what was! The fucking hard-on he'd been sporting since the moment he saw Lyric was making *him* miserable!

Goddamn, she made his blood boil, and his cock feel like it would spew lava when he finally pushed inside her cunt and came.

"Look, I've got connections you don't have. You have contacts that I don't have. It makes sense to join forces." That was as close to reasonable as he was willing to get. She'd find out soon enough who was going to be in control of this investigation—him. He was the cop. He was going to call the shots. And they weren't going to play fast and loose with the law. Forcing a calmness he didn't feel into his voice, he said, "We can go check out Surbeck's place together, or separately. Your choice."

Chapter Three

Lyric hesitated for all of one minute before giving in. Her gut told her that they didn't have much time before the dogs would disappear—permanently. And what he said about working together made sense—not that she couldn't read the writing on the wall. He was in for trouble if he thought he was going to turn this into *his* investigation.

"Fine, let's go."

Gene Surbeck's address turned out to be in an apartment complex, a collection of ugly, blocky buildings with peeling paint and plenty of borrowed shopping carts straddling the curbs. The name G. Surbeck showed up in a crude scrawl above the mailbox for apartment 15-C, Building Three. Kieran led the way up two flights of stairs, confidence rolling off him like a wake behind a barge.

The TV in 15-C was turned way up, probably to drown out the sound of a yelling kid. But Kieran's knock sounded official enough that the noise level dropped and the door opened just wide enough for Lyric to get a look at the woman inside. Her face was heavily made-up, but no amount of bottled goop was going to hide the damage—puffy eye, split lip.

"Yeah, what-da-ya want?"

"You Linda?" Kieran asked.

"Not likely. If you're looking for her, you're a year too late."

"Actually we're looking for some dogs," Lyric said.

The woman's smile turned sly. "I got one here. I might be interested in parting with her." She stepped back to let them in.

The place stunk of urine, cigarettes, and beer. A little boy with no clothing wandered in from another room and peed on the carpet in front of the TV. The woman reached over and gave the toddler a whack on his butt. "Not on the carpet!"

The boy started bawling. The woman knelt down next to the sofa and reached under, grabbing until she caught a hind leg and managed to get a protesting mass of filthy white fur out from under the couch. "Here she is." The woman huffed to her feet. "Her real name is Ant-wa-nette. But we just call her Lady."

Lyric held out her arms for the dog. The woman relinquished her without a word, then lit a cigarette and sucked in a lungful of smoke. "I got her a while back. She was real cute and fancy when we brought her home. But I don't have no time to cut her hair and give her baths. Besides, she didn't take to Frankie." The woman waved her cigarette in the direction of the still crying child. "Guess she's never been around kids. Mainly she just stays under the couch."

Lyric's skin tingled with the sixth sense she'd learned to trust. "Where'd you get her?"

"She followed me home from the grocery store." The woman giggled. "I just put her in the basket with the rest of my things and brought her home—kind of like a present to myself."

"I didn't know there was a grocery store in walking distance."

"Well, it ain't close. But I go to the Safeway over on San Carlos—usually cut through the Rose Garden to get there."

Lyric nodded. The Rose Garden was an old neighborhood of beautifully maintained houses with a park in its center that had hundreds of different rose varieties in it. "Is that where you found Lady, in the Rose Garden?"

The sly expression appeared again. The woman shook her head. "Tell you the truth, I don't remember any more. Gene'd know, but he ain't here right now."

Kieran shifted. "He the one who hit you?"

The sly expression disappeared, followed by a suspicious one. Lyric tried to divert the woman. "How much do you want for Lady?"

The woman took another long pull on her cigarette and looked at Lyric, then Kieran. "Fifty bucks."

Kieran snorted. "For that fleabag?"

Lyric shot him a warning look. He might be trying to haggle down to a cheaper price, but she wasn't willing to risk losing the dog. She'd bet twice the fifty that somebody in the Rose Garden was missing a well-loved pet.

Lyric moved closer to Kieran, angling so she could press against his thigh and give her aching pussy some relief while clueing him in on how this was going to go. "I'm going to be mad at you if I can't take Lady home with me." She felt his cock jump against her leg and couldn't resist rubbing against him just enough to see his eyes flash with lust.

Son of bitch but she was asking for it. Braden was right when he said his little hellion of a cousin needed a man to set some rules and enforce them. Two could play this game. Kieran speared his fingers through her hair and forced her face to his. "I'll buy the dog, but you're going to pay me back, baby, and I don't take cash."

Heat flashed through Lyric's body at his show of dominance. She couldn't resist answering his challenge. "Whatever you say, Kieran."

His smile was feral as he loosened his grip on her hair and managed to brush his hand against her aroused nipple when he reached for his wallet. Lyric only barely held back a moan as she turned toward the woman.

She didn't think Gene Surbeck had Anna's dogs, but she wanted to try and verify that before they left. "You sure it's going to be okay with your...husband...if I take the dog?"

The woman waved the cigarette in the air though her eyes remained locked on the dollar bills emerging from Kieran's wallet. "Gene don't care. He'd sell his own kid if it'd raise his bail money."

"He's in jail?" Lyric asked.

The woman actually licked her lips as Kieran offered her the money. But when she would have taken if from him, he held tight and said, "Just so we know there's not going to be a problem, Gene's in jail?"

The woman's eyes flickered to Kieran's face and then back to the money. She shrugged. "Yeah, cops came and got him day before yesterday."

Kieran opened his hand and she snatched the dollar bills. Lyric turned and left the apartment. When they got to her Jeep she said, "You going to have Child Protective Services check up on the kid?"

He nodded and extended his hand. "Keys. I'm not holding the dog."

"That's why I have crates in the Jeep." She unlocked the car and put the dog in a crate in the rear. Kieran moved in behind her and trapped her body between the Jeep and his. She shivered when his hand came around and rested on her abdomen, just above the waistband of her jeans.

Kieran's lips brushed against her neck. "Baby, if you think I'm going to let you tease me and get away with it, then you've been playing with the wrong kind of men."

His fingers dipped below the waistband of her pants and she couldn't stop the involuntary clench of her stomach that made a hollow pathway right down to where she needed his touch the most. This time his lips sucked at the skin of her neck as he pressed his erection against her back and let his hand slide down inside her panties.

As soon as he hit the bare flesh, his hips gave an involuntary thrust and his breath came out in a pant. *Son of a bitch.*

Fire ripped through Kieran's cock and up his spine. Fuck. She was his favorite fantasy—the one thing he hadn't dared ask any of his casual sex partners to do because he knew that once he experienced a bare pussy, he'd never be able to go back.

Goddamn, he wanted to rip her jeans down and see the mound his fingers were touching. He wanted to bury his face in her cunt and lick and suck until she was screaming and begging for him to fuck her. And then he wanted to bend her over the front of the car and shove his cock into her.

Shit. If he'd known she was going to be smooth and soft and so fucking wet, he'd have waited to push his hand into her panties. One wriggle of her tight little ass and he was going to come in his pants. Fuck—then the little hellion would know she had him.

He closed his eyes against the white-hot need. The only way to do this was to make a clean break. His cock pulsed in protest and his hips gave another involuntary thrust.

Kieran jerked away and stepped back but the scent of her arousal followed him. The feel of it, slick on his fingers, made him want to bring his hand to his lips and taste her, to free his penis and smear her juices on it.

Lyric closed her eyes and concentrated on not panting, not pleading, and not pleasuring herself right where she stood. Oh God, she was in such trouble. But at least they'd left Kieran's Harley at Anna's place. If they'd left it at his, she'd end up with her legs spread and his cock deep and hard inside of her. She needed to take a step back and think before she let that happen. It was one thing to fantasize about finding a man who could thoroughly dominate her—it was a whole other thing to actually experience the reality. No way was she going to turn over the car keys. Right now they were the only things keeping her in control of the situation.

Lyric straightened and moved away, opening the door and slipping into the driver's seat. Without a word she unlocked the other side. The muscle in Kieran's jaw twitched. *Fine, baby, you can pretend that you're in control all you want, but you're going to learn differently.*

They made the drive to Anna's house in silence though the air in the car pulsed with heated, unspoken exchanges. Lyric parked behind his Harley. "I've got to take the dog home and get it cleaned up."

His fingers curled around the nape of her neck, forcing her to face him. "I'll follow you."

"That's not a good idea."

Kieran's eyes narrowed. He reached for one of her hands and pressed it against his erection. Heat seared her palm and spread to her nipples and clit. She whimpered.

"Yeah, baby, you're going to be doing a lot of that." He rubbed her hand along the thick ridge. She closed her eyes against the lust rushing through her.

"Kieran…" Her eyes flew open at the feel of wet, silky skin. He'd unzipped his jeans and freed a few inches of his penis. Her breath caught at the sight of its hungry thickness. As she watched, more liquid escaped from the slit in its dark head.

He pressed closer so that his mouth hovered above hers. "We can do this the easy way or the hard way, baby." His tongue traced the seam of her lips. "The easy way is I give you enough time to go into Grandma's house and get the dog cleaned up, then we leave it here and go to my place."

His tongue delved into her mouth and there was no way to hide her response. She opened wider, tangling her tongue with his in a frantic imitation of sex. They were both breathing hard when he pulled back. "The hard way is I follow you home, but as soon as you get out of your car, I'm going to get you inside your place and fuck you. While I do that, your little rescue project is going to be waiting in her little jail until I get finished. And trust me on this, baby, it's going to be a long time before I get done with you."

Kieran moved in again and covered her lips with his, but this time as his tongue mated with hers, he forced her hand to slide up and down his penis. Lyric whimpered, desperate to feel more of their bodies touching, desperate for relief.

He pulled away again, his face tight with need, his eyes dilated. "Make a decision, baby."

She licked her lips and his cock jerked in her hand. "I'll leave the dog here."

"Good choice." His eyes didn't leave hers as he moved her hand up and down his shaft one more time. "Just a warning, baby, if you try and run later, I'll cuff you and turn your ass red before I fuck you."

Lyric shivered and closed her eyes as dark fantasies rushed over her. Kieran's husky laugh whispered across her cheek as he released her.

Somehow Lyric managed to act normal when they walked into Anna's house. It helped that Kieran immediately disappeared into the TV room and left them to deal with the dog.

Lyric smiled as she watched Kieran's grandmother fussing over the dog as she dried its hair with the blow dryer. This had been a good idea. It gave Anna something to occupy her thoughts.

"Almost dry?" Lyric asked.

"Just about."

"I'd like to give her a haircut and turn her back into a poodle before I leave."

Anna's face showed her surprise. "A poodle? I never would have guessed. Are you sure?" She laughed and it lightened Lyric's heart. "Of course you're sure. This is your business."

"Well, I've got a little advantage when it comes to poodles. My very first dog was a miniature poodle. Ultimately I made friends with a woman doing poodle rescue. She'd get them in looking worse than this one does. There were times I'd swear that she'd finally been fooled. But a bath and a haircut and the dogs always turned out to be poodles."

They moved to the laundry room where Anna had a table that lent itself to grooming. A short time later, Lady, the terrorized mess, was transformed to what she'd probably looked like the day she ended up at Gene Surbeck's apartment—Antoinette, someone's beautiful miniature poodle.

Anna stroked the little dog's head. "What will you do next?"

"Go online to the newspaper archives and see if I can find a 'lost pet' ad. If that doesn't work, then I'll swing by the animal shelters and see if anyone posted a missing pet notice, and after that, local veterinarians. All the places I've got to hit once I make up posters for your three."

Anna's hand shook at the mention of her missing pets. "Do you think you'll find them?"

"I don't know." Lyric reached over and placed her hand on Anna's. "But I will do anything I can to get them back." *Including breaking the law.*

Kieran's cock jumped as he stopped in the doorway and heard the unspoken part of Lyric's promise. *Yeah, baby, you might think you've got free rein to do anything you want, but you're going to learn differently. Starting now.* "Ready?" he asked, startling both women.

His grandmother's smile sent a rush of pure warmth through his heart. Damn, he'd been worried about her.

Lyric's wary expression sent a bolt of fire straight to his cock. *Oh yeah, you should be worried.* Fuck, he needed to get her out of here.

"Can you believe this is the same dog?" his grandmother asked and Kieran forced his attention away from Lyric. He blinked, taking in the changes in the dog.

"She looks good." His grandmother frowned and Kieran knew she was getting ready to lecture him. "I mean she looks great. Like a new dog." He looked at his watch. "Lyric and I need to hit the road."

His grandmother's frown held for a moment longer before she nodded and asked, "Is there anything I can do to help?"

Lyric gave Anna's hand a little squeeze. "Just taking care of Antoinette is a big help. That'll free me up."

They left a few minutes later. When they got to the Jeep, Kieran wrapped his fingers around Lyric's arm. "Keys."

She shivered at the dominant tone, at the dark promise of retribution if she didn't submit. Every nerve ending in her body responded to it, was thrilled by it, craved it.

Chapter Four

Goddamn, he was in trouble. He'd never had it this bad for a woman. Never felt like he would do just about anything to get one underneath him.

He'd been working vice for years and had his share of on-duty time in strip joints and whorehouses, but he'd never felt like this. Hadn't even felt like this with any of the women who made it their life's work to hang out in cop bars and offer comfort to the men in blue—and he'd had his share of them, even played rough with some of the ones who wanted it that way.

Christ. The lust pouring through him had just about every drop of blood in his body rushing to his cock—and the real kicker was that it had started with Lyric's first little show of guts, the way she'd moved into his space and not let him intimidate her!

Shit. And then her little hints of defiance…

And the bare pussy… He hadn't even seen it yet and he was having a hard time keeping his mind on the case—on finding his own grandmother's dogs!

He was so hard that the thought of riding his Harley home was enough to make him howl in pain.

If she didn't turn over the keys…

She did, and a fresh rush of lust raged through him.

* * * * *

A cop! What was she thinking of?

He was going to be a complication. Even Bulldog didn't tell her how to run her cases.

Not that she was a big-time lawbreaker, but she'd always had a little trouble accepting that the rules had to protect both the innocent and the guilty.

Lyric shivered as they pulled into a driveway not that many miles from Anna's house. Her body was aching for Kieran, but her mind was screaming for her to run like hell unless she wanted to have her world turned upside down.

Kieran didn't give her a chance to bolt. As soon as the Jeep came to a stop, he had her out of the car and in his house—her back against the inside of the door, her front pressed hard and tight against his body while his mouth covered hers in a kiss that eradicated all thought.

Lyric whimpered and rubbed against his erection, desperate for the feel of skin-on-skin as his hands made short work of opening her shirt and bra, his fingers zeroing in on her nipples, squeezing them in time to the thrusts of his tongue. He pulled away, panting, his face flushed, his eyes dropping immediately to her breasts.

Christ. She was beautiful. The sight of her dark nipples had his balls pulling tight and his cock leaking. Fuck, he'd better get her to his bedroom before he saw any more of her. It was all he could do not to put his mouth on her and start sucking, and once he did that, he wouldn't be able to stay away from her cunt. Kieran almost doubled over as a rush of icy-hot lust whipped through his penis. The thought of the smooth flesh between her thighs sent his hand to the front of his jeans, his fingers tightening around his own cock. Fuck, he was two strokes from coming and there was no way he was going to let that happen. "Let's go, baby," he growled and guided her to his bedroom.

Lyric only had an instant to appreciate the masculine room with its huge bed before Kieran said, "Strip."

She shivered at the feral hunger she saw in his eyes, at the way he stood, legs spread, fingers manipulating his own cock through the fabric of his jeans. When she licked her lips, his nostrils flared and his eyes narrowed.

For a split second she thought about defying him, about saying no and pushing him over the edge, but that'd be too quick, too easy, and that wouldn't prove anything other than the fact that he was bigger, stronger.

She licked her lips again and slowly peeled away her shirt and then her bra, taking a few minutes to linger over her breasts, to cup them and run her thumbs over the engorged tips, letting her body arch suggestively as pleasure rushed through her.

Against his will, Kieran moved into her, crowding her closer to the bed. "Let me see your mouth on them," he growled, his penis jerking painfully when her tongue swirled over first one dark areola and then the other, leaving them wet and glistening.

He leaned over and mimicked what she'd done, satisfaction pouring through him at the way her hands went to his head, holding him to her as she whimpered and arched, silently pleading for more.

"You like that, don't you, baby?"

"Yes." She pressed harder, trying to entice him to do more than just lick.

Kieran took one dark nipple into his mouth, giving it a light suck before releasing it, and moving to the other nipple.

Lyric was shivering with need. "Kieran…"

"Tell me what you want."

"Suck me, bite me."

He straightened and stepped back. "Then do what I told you to do. Strip."

She removed her shoes and socks first, then opened the front of her jeans, flashing the small wedge of black fabric that served as her panties. Kieran tightened his grip on his cloth-covered penis. Lyric's eyes met his as she slowly peeled her jeans down and kicked them off.

"All of it," Kieran growled, the sight of her standing there in the little black thong testing his willpower.

Lyric's laugh was husky, challenging, in perfect harmony with the defiance that danced in her eyes. She stepped forward, her hand joining his as he massaged his cock through his jeans. "You next."

"Oh no, baby, that's not how it's going to work between you and me. Not on the case, and not here in the bedroom. I call the shots. You obey."

"I don't think so."

Kieran wrapped his arm around her waist, holding her in position as he plunged his hand into her panties and zeroed in on her clit with ruthless efficiency. Fire ripped through the tiny nub as he circled and twirled and rubbed.

"Oh god," Lyric whimpered, her arms going around his neck to keep her from sinking to the floor as his touch became her entire reality. Kieran captured her mouth, his tongue demanding entry, stroking in and out in sync with the flashes of searing heat radiating from her clit. When she tried to open her legs wider, to rub harder, to get that little bit of extra friction that would send her over, Kieran pulled his hand away, leaving her shaking with need.

"On no, baby, you're not going to come until I let you. Now strip," he said, releasing her.

Lyric smoothed the tiny strip of black cloth down her legs and Kieran almost doubled over at the sight of the bare, swollen flesh between her legs. "Get on the bed." It came out harsh, guttural.

He unzipped his jeans, peeling them open so that his cock sprang free. As Lyric slid onto the bed, he gripped his penis, stroking it, tempting her with its hard, thick hunger. She felt like she was drowning in lust. Her clit pulsed in time to his strokes. Her cunt clenched, coating her outer lips and inner thighs with wet desire.

"Open your legs, baby."

She opened then, thrilled by the rough edge in his voice, the feral hunger in his eyes. He might think he was in control, but he was as turned-on as she was. She sent him a small challenging smile then reached between her thighs, teasing her clit before slipping two fingers into her aching slit.

He was on her in an instant, wrenching her arms above her head and pinning her wrists to the bed with one hand. "Your cousin, Braden, told me all about you. He said you always pushed, that you just couldn't keep from testing the limits. Well, baby, you can test me all you want, but there're going to be consequences." Before she could guess his intent, Kieran brought his hand down in a firm slap across her pussy.

Shock ripped through Lyric along with scorching pleasure. He struck again, this time angling his hand so that her clit took the impact, shoving icy heat up her spine and into her nipples. She arched upward, desperate, "Oh god, Kieran, please put your mouth on me."

Kieran closed his eyes against the sight of her. Christ, he wasn't sure who was being punished. His balls were heavy and tight, his cock so full that if he wasn't careful, he'd start humping the air like some pathetic dog.

Fuck. He wanted to bury his face between her legs. He wanted to lick and suck and stroke his tongue in and out of her wet slit until she screamed. Instead, he opened his eyes and spanked her smooth cunt again.

Lyric barely recognized herself. She writhed on the edge of orgasm as the slaps came faster, harder, blending pain and pleasure so thoroughly that she couldn't tell the difference any more. No man had ever taken control like this, had ever pushed her to the point that she'd obey any command as long as the sensations bombarding her didn't end.

When he stopped, she cried out, a pleading sound that came from her soul. Kieran released her hands and climbed off the bed. "Scoot up and grab the headboard. Then spread your legs." He stripped out of his clothes and joined her, kneeling between her legs as her fingers wrapped around the smooth wooden dowels in his headboard.

The breath heaved in and out of Kieran's chest as his heart thundered in his ears, threatening to jump out of his chest. Fuck, he felt barely in control but he couldn't afford to show any weakness now — not when he saw surrender in every soft line of her body. "Keep your hands just like that, baby, if you're good then I'll let you come. If you disobey, then I'm going to punish you again."

Lyric could barely breathe as he lowered his head. She wanted to grab his hair and force him down to her cunt, to wrap her legs around him and trap him against her aching flesh, but she didn't dare disobey, not when the promise of relief was so close. She shivered in anticipation, spreading her legs wider and arching slightly, the juices from her channel sliding along the crevice between her buttocks.

She felt desperate, like an animal in heat that wanted to present its vulva to a prospective mate, to rub it over his mouth so that he caught the taste and scent of her and felt driven to mate. At the first swipe of Kieran's tongue over her clit, the first lingering exploration of her channel, Lyric sobbed and began pleading.

Lust overwhelmed Kieran as soon as he buried his face in her cunt. There was no going back now. The taste of her, the smell of her, the sounds she was making as she writhed and bucked and pleaded, begging for him to possess her completely, fiercely, roughly, only fueled his urgent need to master her.

His hands went to her buttocks, holding her firmly in place as his tongue lashed her mercilessly, driving her to orgasm over and over again until she went limp underneath him. Satisfaction ripped through Kieran when he raised his head from her saturated, well-loved cunt and saw that she was still gripping the headboard as he'd ordered, her body soft and submissive.

"That's good, baby," he rubbed his cheek against her pussy, then placed a tender kiss on it before rising to his knees. "See how much better it is when you obey. Now get on your hands and knees."

His demand sent a fresh wave of need through Lyric. Her eyes dropped to his penis and she shivered in anticipation of having him mount her and shove its thick length into her. As soon as she'd complied, Kieran's fingers slipped between her legs, tunneling in and out of her sheath. "You're so tight. I'm going to love pushing in here, feeling you resist before you give in to me. Your cunt's just like you are, baby, you've always got to fight a little at first, until you know you can't win."

He pulled his fingers out and trailed them over the small pucker of her anus. Lyric hunched in reaction. Kieran's laugh was husky and satisfied. "And I'm going to fuck you here, too, baby. Maybe not tonight. But soon." He circled the tight pucker before levering himself over her, kissing and sucking at her neck while one hand reached around to squeeze and torment her nipples.

"I bet you've never let a man do that to you, have you, Lyric, never let a man ram into your ass?"

"No."

"You'll like it. You like a little pain with your pleasure." She dropped her head as he gave her a punishing bite on the shoulder. "I can give you both, baby, pain and pleasure."

His hand trailed lower, going to her clit as the weight of his upper body pressed Lyric's chest to the bed, leaving her buttocks raised, her legs opened, the swollen folds of her cunt exposed, vulnerable—inviting.

Kieran eased back, the erotic image of Lyric offering herself to him seared into his mind for all time. His cock pulsed in warning. Playtime was over. With a groan, he mounted her, shoving all the way in with one rough stroke. The walls of her sheath clamped down on him, sending exquisite pleasure along every nerve ending, trying to hold him in place even as Lyric angled higher, wriggling and pushing back, needing him to thrust, to go deeper and slam into her cervix.

The scorching heat of her channel made him cry out. In an instant of clarity he knew he should pull out, should ask about protection, but some primitive, primal instinct rebelled, taking over so that all he could think about, all that he felt was the furious animal need to rut on his mate and spew his seed into her womb.

His balls slapped against her clit as he slammed into her, dominating, controlling, bringing her to release and savoring every ripple, every tightening of her cunt around his engorged shaft until white fire whipped down his spine, coiling for an endless second in his balls before erupting through his cock in a release so powerful that he knew he would never be the same again.

He collapsed beside Lyric and pulled her tight to his body, his penis still trapped in her wet depths. *Christ, what just happened?* He'd gone in unprotected! Fuck, he was still in her unprotected and he couldn't make himself pull out.

"Tell me you're on the pill, baby."

She tensed in his arms for an instant before relaxing. "I'm on the pill."

He wasn't disappointed, but he didn't feel a rush of relief either and that scared the shit out of him. She snuggled against him, soft and pliant and Kieran's hand smoothed over her bare pussy. Goddamn. He could pet her all day.

Lyric's hand covered his, forcing it to her clit, and his cock jerked, filling with blood so quickly that for a second he felt lightheaded. Her cunt tightened on him in response, quivering and pulsing and drowning him in hot need.

He almost cried out when she moved, forcing his cock out as she rolled to her back. "I want you again," she whispered, her hands going to her nipples as she spread her legs and offered herself to him.

Kieran moved over her, bending his head down and nudging her hand away from one breast. In response she arched upward, her nipple demanding entry against the seam of his lips. Kieran's husky laugh sent a warm gust of air over the sensitive areola. He gave her a painful nip then smoothed it with his tongue, satisfaction raging through him at how responsive she was.

Groaning, he latched onto her nipple, hungry for the taste of her, for the sounds she made when he pleasured her. He wanted to eat her alive, to lick and suck and bite every inch of her body. To claim every part of her—own every part of her.

When her legs wrapped around his waist, he plunged into her. Christ, he never wanted to stop fucking her—never wanted to be more than a few hours away from the wet heat of her.

Chapter Five

Taking a shower might have washed the scent of their lovemaking off Lyric's body, but it didn't lessen the impact of what they'd done together. She shivered under the hot spray of water, worried that she'd never be the same again, that she'd never be able to settle for less than what she'd experienced with him. Oh yeah, she'd known he was trouble the second she saw him. It had taken every bit of willpower she had to slip out of his bed and out of his house without waking him and begging him to fuck her again. She shuddered again, afraid of the need he generated in her.

Until last night, she'd always seen herself as a risk-taker, a live-life-to-the-fullest kind of person who wasn't afraid of getting hurt either physically or emotionally. But what she'd done with Kieran changed that. It made her see that when it came to love, she'd always held back an important piece of herself. True, she didn't think any of her previous partners had known, but how could they? She hadn't even been aware of it herself. There'd been some fun times and creative sex, but looking back on it now, Lyric could see that it was just play—mutually satisfying—but still just a game. What she'd experienced with Kieran was the real deal—she'd never been like that with any man. Never teased and tormented, challenged herself and her partner until the stakes were impossibly high. She'd given herself over to him—completely. It had been intense, beyond belief, and she craved it again. But if she wasn't careful, she was going to end up having her world ripped apart.

Lyric closed her eyes, unable to stop herself from smoothing her hands over her breasts. The nipples were still so sensitive. She rolled them between her fingers, tugging and twisting and remembering Kieran's mouth, his touch.

One hand slid to her cunt, its fingers stroking her clit and sending fire streaking down to her toes. Her womb clenched and heat flared through her labia as she remembered his punishing slaps to her pussy.

He'd been everything she'd ever dreamed of in a lover. A man who could totally dominate her sexually.

She increased the pressure on her clit, imagining it was his tongue and hearing the sounds of his sucking, his moaning as he'd devoured her. With a small shudder she came just enough to ease some of the tension. Oh god, she was in such big trouble.

Lyric moved from the shower then, drying herself and getting dressed. The only hope she had of getting her life back under control was to concentrate on Anna's case and to spend some time getting the poodle back to its real owner.

She started with the online archives for the local paper and went back to the previous Christmas. The holiday season was the perfect time for animals to go missing—especially if a house was full of guests not used to paying attention to open doors. And Surbeck's girlfriend had made the comment about Ant-wa-nette being a present to herself.

A few minutes later, Lyric had what she was looking for. "Jackpot."

Poodle. White miniature female. Rose Garden area. Missing since 12/24. Owner devastated. Reward offered, no questions asked.

Lyric picked up the phone and made the call, praying that one day she'd be able to make the same call to Anna and to John Merriman. She wasn't surprised to learn that Antoinette had escaped on Christmas Eve when one of Mrs. Abbot's grandchildren had accidentally left the door open. The poodle had been wearing a collar with tags on it, and while ninety-nine percent of the population would have returned the dog immediately, Antoinette ended up with a member of the one percent who wouldn't—and didn't. Lyric sent Mrs. Abbot to Anna's house without mentioning the fifty dollars that Kieran had laid out. She figured he'd more than gotten his money's worth.

* * * * *

Son of a bitch. She was gone. He didn't fucking believe it.

Kieran wrapped a hand around his penis. His cock was as hard as a steel pole and he wanted her again.

Goddamn. She'd slipped out like he was some fucking one-night stand that she didn't want to face in the morning light.

She wouldn't make that mistake again.

* * * * *

The phone rang just as Lyric finished cropping and pasting a picture of Anna's dachshunds into a "Stolen Dogs" flyer on her computer. Her hand hovered over the phone for a second, her heart pounding at the thought it might be Kieran, then she shook her head and picked up the receiver. *Get a grip!*

"Lyric, this is John Merriman. I'm sorry if I woke you, but Emily's been found! She's on her way home."

"That's fantastic news, John! Where and when?"

"She was found last Tuesday by a trucker who was in the area. He called me today from Florida. It turns out that he found her a couple of blocks away from where I live. She was on Benton, it's about an eight-minute walk from my house! He couldn't stop to try and find an owner, so he took her with him, figuring he'd do the best he could for her. Then a friend of his saw one of my reward posters and gave him a call. That's how he got my number. It's got to be her. He described her perfectly. The reward poster didn't show the nick in her ear, but the trucker described it to me."

Oh no. Lyric's excitement plummeted to despair. "John, did the trucker ask for money? Did he say that he's short of funds, but would be happy to ship the dog back if you sent a money order?"

A painful silence greeted her question. In a much-subdued voice, John said, "Yes. He said that he didn't want the reward. But if I sent the five hundred immediately then he'd be able to get her on a redeye flight. He said that he would have to get a health certificate from the vet, which would run about fifty. Then the plane ticket would be about four-fifty since it's an unaccompanied dog traveling on short notice."

"Did he give you a telephone number where he could be reached? Anything that would prove he's legitimate?"

Silence again. "No, he said that he was just laying over in Miami, picking up more cargo, but the shipper moved the time up, so now he was in a real bind to get Emily taken care of." John drew a deep breath. "He called from a payphone at the airport, right after he put Emily on the plane."

Lyric rubbed her forehead, pissed and heartsick. If she could put a bullet through the guy running this scam, she would. "You sent the money?"

"Yes. Yes, right away. Luckily I had the cash on hand. I got it from the bank the day I put the reward posters up."

"When did you send the money?"

"Late last night, right after he called. He had to have it before he took her to the airport." John hesitated. "I'm sure it's her. It's got to be her. And even if it's not, I'll try and find the owner. If I can't do that, then I'll provide a good home for her."

"Have you checked with the airline to see if there's a flight in from Miami?"

"Yes. It'll be here in an hour."

"Did you verify how much it would cost to ship a dog?"

"No. I didn't care. Ernie sounded so nice. He seemed to really care about dogs. He even told me all about his dogs and how much he misses them when he's on the road. I would have given him the shipping costs and the five hundred dollar reward if he'd asked me to."

Lyric closed her eyes. "Is it okay if I come with you to the airport?"

Perceptive silence greeted her question. "You're afraid she won't on the plane."

"I've read about scams that play out like this."

"But you've never actually known anyone who was a victim?" His voice held a mix of hope and despair.

"No, I haven't personally known anyone who was a victim of this scam. But it's a popular one and it surfaces from time to time. Is it okay if I go to the airport with you?"

He hesitated for a long moment before saying, "I'd like that."

Lyric grabbed the case file she'd started along with the fliers she'd printed out while they were talking and left the house.

John Merriman's house was a small stucco home with a Spanish tile roof and a yard full of flowers. He opened the door before Lyric could ring the bell and said, "I thought you might want a cup of coffee before we left for the airport."

"That'd be great, thanks." She followed him inside, guessing that he was about Anna's age. His haggard face and the dark circles under his eyes concerned Lyric.

Like Anna's house, John's home was a testament to his status as a grandparent. There were pictures of children and grandchildren, and a huge collection of child-made crafts. And like the yard, there were flowers everywhere.

"I thought we could have our coffee in the kitchen. The plants have kind of taken over. There's no room on the coffee table for drinks or snacks anymore."

John waved in the direction of the kitchen table. "Go ahead and sit down, help yourself to a cookie. I'll bring the coffee over."

There was a plate of cookies on the table as well as a couple of coffee mugs. The mugs sported pictures of dachshunds. John poured the coffee and sat down.

A stack of photos rested in the center of the table. "Emily?" Lyric asked.

He nodded and looked away, but not before she saw the moisture in his eyes. She looked through the pictures as she drank her coffee. One in particular caught her eye. It was a profile that clearly showed the distinguishing tear in the dog's ear. "She's beautiful. Can I keep this photo for a while?"

He reached over and rubbed his finger along the edge of the photograph almost as though he were stroking the dog. "Of course. Keep it for as long as you need." He got up and retrieved some reward fliers from the counter. "Take these as well." The uncertainty about whether or not Emily would be on the plane hung silent between them.

"We can take my car," Lyric finally said.

John nodded, looking very much like a frail old man.

Chapter Six

Kieran didn't know whether to be pissed or relieved that the poodle was gone. One minute his grandmother was laughing and recounting what had happened when Antoinette's owner arrived, and then in the next breath, she was worrying about her dachshunds and crying.

Shit. He didn't know how to cope with a crying woman—especially one he loved. "Grandma, you're going to make yourself sick. Please stop."

She didn't.

He speared his fingers through his hair. Fuck, this was a nightmare. "Is Lyric coming by today?"

For some unknown female reason, that stopped the tears. He understood a second later after she'd wiped her eyes and given him a speculative look. "You two seemed to be getting along last night when you brought Antoinette over. In fact, I got the impression that maybe you were... She's a lovely person, isn't she?"

Kieran turned away, embarrassed by the flood of color that washed across his face. Fuck! Had she noticed the woody he was sporting last night or was she just matchmaking? She'd been trying to get her grandsons settled for years now. He'd escaped to the TV room so it wouldn't be so obvious—but short of cupping his hands in front of his groin, it wasn't like he could hide Lyric's effect on him.

Shit! And just where the fuck was Lyric? What part of "we're working this case together" didn't she understand? When he caught up to her...

And now he had to dodge his grandmother's questions. He looked at his watch and said, "The artist should be here in a few minutes. Tyler might be a coffee drinker and the stuff at the station'll rot your guts."

Because Kieran was still turned away, he didn't see the gleam in his grandmother's eye or the smile on her face. If he had, even more color would have raced to his face.

"I'll go make some right now," Anna said, laughing silently as she moved toward the kitchen. The house had been a furnace last night with the heat generated between Kieran and Lyric. Oh, she recognized it well enough—remembered the heady rush of love and lust that she'd experienced with Kieran's grandfather, God rest his soul. She chuckled. No doubt her grandson would be shocked to know that she understood passion!

One grandson down—though Kieran was just stubborn enough to fight it—two more to go. Anna 's heart warmed. She'd have some great-grandbabies to look after yet!

Tyler Keane was not at all what Anna had expected, and she found herself hoping that Lyric wouldn't arrive while he was there. Not that she thought Kieran suffered in comparison to the police artist—not at all. Her grandson was a wonderful man and any woman would be lucky to have him...but, well, Tyler was just absolutely stunning.

There, she'd admitted it to herself. She might be a grandmother, but that didn't mean there were no hormones in her system—and in another day, Tyler, with his long, golden locks, might have been a dashing buccaneer. Not that Kieran couldn't have played the part, too…but, well, her grandson would have to play a much darker role. He didn't have the easy charm that Tyler did. With smiles that washed over Anna like a spring shower and words that had eased her through the painful memory of reliving the theft of her dogs, Tyler had managed to pull the image of her attacker right out of her mind.

"That's him," Anna said, shivering at the likeness that appeared on Tyler's computer.

Tyler reached over and squeezed her hand. "You did great, Mrs. Simmons. Just great."

Anna's heart fluttered at the contact. Tyler smiled and she could see it went soul-deep. What a marvelous man!

Kieran shifted in his seat and drew Anna's attention away from the artist. Her grandson was frowning. He looked so much like his grandfather—God rest his soul—when he did that. "What will you do next?" she asked him.

"Run it through a computer program and see if we get a match."

Tyler shook his head. "No need. I saw a flier on this guy a couple of weeks ago. Caught my eye because he's got an interesting face—simple lines, brutal." A few keystrokes later and the information about Harry Rickard was on his screen.

Kieran grunted. "Great. He escaped from Lompoc Federal Penitentiary. How the hell did that happen?"

Tyler adjusted the data. "Looks like he was in a knife fight and got injured. Officials thought it was bad enough to take him to a local hospital. He repaid them by overpowering two guards and escaping. The two guards had to be hospitalized."

"Son of a bitch."

Reflexively, Anna said, "Kieran…"

"Sorry, Grandma." Kieran turned back and scowled at Tyler who was doing nothing to hide his amusement. "What's Rickard in for?"

"Armed robbery. Held up a convenience store—shot two people, both survived. Been in and out of jail most of his adult life. Looks like a real winner."

Anna rested a hand on Tyler's arm. "Could you print this information out, along with his picture? I'd like a copy."

"Grandma," Kieran warned, already guessing where her copy was going to go. The last thing he wanted was for Lyric to chase after a guy like Rickard.

* * * * *

Lyric didn't want to leave John at his house alone—not that he'd be able to outrun his hurt and anger at being conned, or the crushing disappointment of not getting his dog back—but at least she could give him some people-time to ease the burden. So she'd played upon his desire to help someone and talked him into coming to Anna's house with her.

What she hadn't counted on was finding Kieran's car parked in front. The cherried-out muscle machine was hard to miss or forget, especially when the last time she'd seen it, it was parked in Kieran's drive and she was sneaking away from his house. Shit, she'd really wanted to avoid him for a couple of days. But now that she'd gotten this far, there was no turning back.

"Anna's grandson is a vice cop. If you feel up to it, you should tell him what happened," Lyric said as they made their way up the sidewalk. John nodded but didn't respond otherwise.

Anna seemed flustered by the sight of John and Lyric on her doorstep. "Is this a bad time?" Lyric asked.

"No. No, come on in. It's actually very good timing. We know who took my dogs!"

Lyric introduced John to Anna as they stepped into the house, but before she could ask more about Anna's dogs, a flush of surprised pleasure washed over her. "Tyler!"

Possessive rage roared through Kieran as Tyler moved from his seat on the couch into a body-pressing hug with Lyric. When their lips touched, it was just about all Kieran could do to keep from stomping over and wrenching the other man away from his woman—Son of a bitch! His thoughts screeched to a halt. His woman? His cock pulsed with angry need. Yeah. His woman. Maybe he hadn't made that clear enough to her last night.

Tyler and Lyric broke apart. Tyler said, "I should have known this was one of your cases."

Lyric laughed and it sent another round of fury through Kieran. Goddamn, he didn't like the thought of that husky laugh curling around another man's cock.

"What are you doing here, Ty?" Lyric asked.

Tyler grinned and Kieran's eyes narrowed, silently daring Lyric's nipples to go to tight points underneath her shirt. He'd seen the way women fell at Tyler's feet. Fuck, even his grandmother had been charmed.

"If you can't beat 'em, join 'em."

Lyric's eyes widened. "You're a cop? This is the mystery job you wouldn't tell me anything about?"

"Police artist." Tyler grinned again. "Though I prefer the title Image Recapture Specialist."

It took Lyric a minute to pull her thoughts together and then she experienced a different kind of excitement at finding Tyler here. No one was better at this kind of thing than Tyler. He had people skills plus incredible talent. "So what have you got on the guy who took Anna's dogs?"

"It's on the table. Sorry to say, I've got to head out. I just squeezed this appointment in during a break." He retrieved his laptop and printer, then stopped next to Lyric, brushing a soft kiss against her mouth. "Be careful with this one, doll."

A fresh round of possessive fury raged through Kieran. Son of a bitch, that was twice Tyler had kissed his woman. "I'll walk you out," Kieran growled, pleased to see a flash of worry in Lyric's eyes before they narrowed.

Tyler's gaze moved between Lyric and Kieran. Kieran could see the exact instant the other man put it together. Good. Maybe he wouldn't be forced to pound the shit out of Tyler. The department tended to take a dim view of stuff like that.

As soon as they cleared the front door, Kieran said, "Stay away from her."

Tyler coughed back a laugh. Oh yeah—those two were perfect for each other. He could have told Kieran that Lyric was a childhood friend—that they'd played doctor together and experimented—but they'd never actually fucked—but what the hell? Kieran was all worked up and Lyric would probably enjoy being on the receiving end, so why ruin it for her? "Hey, no problem."

Anna bit her lip to keep from smiling as her grandson stalked back in. He'd be mortified to know just how obvious his feelings were to anyone who knew him. And Lyric, she was doing a wonderful job of ignoring him. Anna forced backed a laugh. Oh, she'd used the same tactics on Kieran's grandfather—God rest his soul—and it had been like waving a red flag in front of a bull.

Anna distracted Kieran long enough to introduce John, then settled back and waited for the inevitable confrontation as Kieran came to a halt next to Lyric and reached for the information Tyler had left. "Don't even think about looking for Rickard. This is police business and if you get involved, I'll lock you up."

Lyric's eyebrows lifted but she didn't release the papers. "Why don't we discuss this later."

A muscle jumped in Kieran's cheek. "Let go of the papers." His voice was a low, dominant growl.

Lyric's nipples tightened at the tone. If they were alone… She shivered. No—not a good idea. "Get serious, Kieran. You can't keep this information from me."

Goddamn! Did she have any idea what her defiance did to him? His cock jumped as images from the previous night flashed through his mind. Oh yeah. She knew.

It killed him to drop his hand away from the papers. Fuck, the last thing he wanted to do was have her go looking for Tyler. He'd called in a few favors to get the artist out here, but Kieran didn't know the man well enough to trust him to resist giving Lyric what she wanted. "Fine, keep the papers, but I'm warning you again—stay away from Rickard." *And as soon as I get you alone, I'm going to drive that point home.* His cock pulsed in anticipation of being used as the messenger.

Chapter Seven

Lyric wasn't optimistic that putting up the "Stolen Dogs" fliers would provide any leads, but it was ground that had to be covered—and it gave Anna and John something useful to do. She smiled as she watched them drive away.

After the initial awkwardness caused by Kieran's little macho fit had dissipated, Anna and John had actually found they had a lot in common and Lyric was willing to bet that they'd be seeing more of each other—even after their dogs had been recovered. Apparently Kieran had the same thought and it wasn't sitting too well with him. He was scowling after his grandmother's car even before he turned that same expression on Lyric. Her womb pulsed, flooding her panties as she braced herself for a rant.

Kieran grabbed her upper arms and jerked her up against his body. She shivered at the feral look in his eyes, at the feel of his erection, at the furious sexual heat he generated. "Rule number one, baby—you do not get out of bed and sneak out of my house. That will fucking piss me off every time. Rule number two—I'm in charge of this case. If I say stay away from parts of it, you better keep the fuck away. And rule three—you belong to me and I don't fucking share—not even kisses. The only thing saving you from feeling my hand on your ass right now is that I've got to go down to the station."

He bent his head and gave Lyric a punishing kiss that demanded nothing less than her total submission. God, it was too much. She couldn't fight both her own fantasies and him. Her body softened, her clit stabbed at the unyielding material of her jeans, and she widened her legs, rubbing against his cloth-covered erection like a cat in heat.

Kieran's hands moved to her hips, adding his strength so that the friction being generated was so exquisite that Lyric wanted to thrash and moan and scream at the sensations coursing through every nerve ending. He pulled his lips from hers and whispered, "That's right, baby, you like a little pain with your pleasure and I'm the man to give you what you want. Tell me you understand the rules and I'll make you come."

Lyric rubbed her nipples against his chest. God, this was so decadent—they were still standing in front of Anna's house—but she was close to coming and she needed it so badly. Kieran's husky laugh washed over her a second before he sucked her earlobe into his mouth and sent piercing heat right to her nipples. One of his hands moved upward, pushing under her shirt and bra to circle and tease an engorged areola. "Tell me that you understand the rules, baby, and I'll bring you off." His fingers finally captured the nipple, squeezing hard enough that Lyric bucked against him, but not hard enough to bring her to orgasm.

Oh God. She couldn't hold out. Any second now and she'd be ripping her shirt up and begging him to bite and suck her. "I understand the rules," she gasped.

His mouth returned to her ear and his tongue fucked in and out of the sensitive canal in time to the fingers squeezing her areola. Lyric's clit felt like it was going to explode as she pumped against his erection. Each strike brought her closer to orgasm, but she didn't go over until he whispered, "Now, baby, come now and I'll only punish you a little bit later."

She sunk her teeth into his shoulder in order to keep from screaming as waves of agonizing pleasure consumed her. His erection surged twice against her clit before he groaned, "Oh shit," and shook with his own release.

Son of a bitch. Kieran buried his hands in Lyric's back pockets so she couldn't see them shake—fuck, so he couldn't see them shake. Goddamn. He'd come in his pants like some fucking teenager with no control.

Shit, his only hope of salvaging this situation was that she'd been too far gone to notice—but when she rubbed her face against his chest like a contented cat then looked up with a knowing smile, he knew he wasn't going to be that lucky. There was just the barest hint of a challenge when she said, "I should get going."

Kieran's eyes narrowed. The little hellion was silently daring him to ask where she was going and what she'd be doing, knowing that the longer he stood out there, the more obvious the wet stain on his pants was going to get. A muscle twitched in his cheek. He speared his fingers through her hair and gave the slightest pull, reminding her that he was in charge. "I'll see you tonight."

Maybe hovered on Lyric's lips, but she didn't give in to the temptation to openly challenge him. This little encounter had ended in a draw—the next one might not. She shrugged, as though she viewed his comment as a suggestion and not a command. "Okay, see you later."

For a long moment, Kieran thought about dragging her into his grandmother's house and fucking her senseless. His cock twitched, ready to rise to the occasion. Goddamn, but she was becoming an obsession. He forced his thoughts away from what he wanted to do to her with the promise that he would do it, later, when he had her in his home, in his bed, and at his mercy.

* * * * *

Lyric went to Crime Tells. Bulldog was out interviewing a potential client, but her sisters were there, playing a game of Liar's Dice.

"Join us?" Erin asked, shifting the blonde braid from one shoulder to the next.

"No, I'm working a case but wanted some company. You guys keep playing, I've got to do some research on the 'net."

Cady shook her head and sent rich brown curls everywhere. "Hey, three people working makes it more fun. What've you got?"

Lyric sat down at the table and filled them in on the case. When she was done, Cady gave a little whistle. "Not your usual case of dognapping."

Erin frowned. "This Harry Rickard worries me, Lyric. Maybe you should see if Grandpa would free up Braden or Shane to help on the case."

Lyric grimaced. "No thanks! One macho man trying to take charge is plenty!"

That got her sisters' attention. "What macho man?" Cady asked.

Heat rushed to Lyric's face. Shit! She hadn't meant to tell them about Kieran. "I guess I didn't mention that Anna's grandson is a vice cop."

Cady and Erin exchanged glances and Lyric knew she hadn't fooled them for a second. Cady grinned. "Okay, give. Don't hold out on us. He's drop-dead gorgeous isn't he?"

"Yeah."

"A to-die-for-alpha-type, fantasy material, right?" Erin said.

Lyric shifted uncomfortably as memories of just how dominant Kieran was flooded her mind and her pussy. "Okay, yeah, he is."

Cady gave another little whistle. "You're in trouble then, aren't you?"

Lyric's breath exited on a long heartfelt sigh. "Yeah, I'm in trouble—big trouble."

Her response caused another silent exchange of glances between Cady and Erin, only this time they both looked concerned. Lyric decided it was better to head them off before they went all "big sister" on her. "If I can get this case solved, then that'll give me some space to figure out what to do about Kieran."

There was a short, heavy silence and Lyric knew that they didn't want to let the subject drop but finally Cady said, "Okay, you're lead on this one—what do you want us to look for?"

Warmth swamped Lyric. Damn she was lucky to have such great sisters. Even when they were kids they'd gotten along like best friends. "I want to e-mail all the dachshund rescue people we can find both in California and Nevada—a lot of times when dogs get lost, the owners will contact rescue—then I want to check newspaper archives for missing, stolen, found and free-to-good-home dachshunds."

"Time frame?" Cady asked.

Lyric nibbled on her bottom lip. "Let's start with the last three months. I think the activity is going to be closer in. My gut tells me that the call just went out and it requires a quick turnaround time or they wouldn't be moving so fast to collect the dogs."

"You're thinking puppy-mill operation or dogs wanted for research?" Erin asked.

"Yeah."

Cady frowned. "John and Anna's dogs would be worthless to a puppy mill. I'll buy that Rickard probably can't tell if a dog is spayed, but he's a guy, he'd notice if a dog didn't have any nuts."

Lyric shook her head. "Believe it or not, there are people who don't know enough to tell if a dog is neutered or not, but it's not as simple as that. Rickard doesn't have the smarts to be behind this kind of operation—he's more of a shove a gun in someone's face or beat them up and take their money kind of a criminal. And even at that, he's not too good or he wouldn't keep getting caught."

"And released," Erin grumbled. "What's wrong with *that* picture?"

Cady and Lyric grinned at each other. Erin had been on the police force for all of one year before she got sick of arresting the same crooks over and over again.

"You were saying?" Cady prompted.

"I was saying that Rickard is probably just hired muscle." Lyric's sixth sense hummed that she was on the right track as she made the next leap. "I'm guessing that they're not after puppy-mill breeders specifically, but that whoever's behind this is either trying to meet a bulk contract or is gathering them together to take to an auction and sell or move them to a middleman."

Erin's eyebrows drew together. "What kind of auction? Where?"

"They're usually in the mid-west, but they can be anywhere. The traders gather and sell what they've accumulated to biological firms, teaching hospitals, research organizations, places like that." Lyric was getting pissed—and worried—just thinking about it. "End users don't ask where the dogs and cats come from. They're disposable and there's a ready supply. And once they get into the system, no one is looking to 'find' someone's pet."

Erin felt sick to her stomach. "Let me guess. There are rules and regulations out there, but nobody around to enforce them."

Lyric shrugged. "Something like that, though sometimes it's more of a case of no willpower instead of no manpower."

Cady's expression turned fierce. "Then let's see what we can do to stop Harry Rickard and fellow scum."

A little while later, they'd found fifteen missing dogs and one that had been stolen when a nine-year-old boy tied his dog's leash outside a convenience store while he went in to get some candy. As he was paying the cashier, the boy looked up and saw a man pick up his dog. The boy yelled and the man took off, too fast for anyone to get a good description.

"Damn, that's a lot of dogs," Cady said. "Especially if you add them to the ones you already know about."

Erin was frowning. "The trouble is, we've got information—mainly a confirmation that someone's collecting dogs—but no leads and no way of knowing what the magic number is before they get bunched together and shipped off somewhere."

Cady picked up a deck of cards from next to the computer and started shuffling. Somehow the smooth feel of the cards being rearranged always helped her think. "John's missing dog fits the crime MO—he walks the dog regularly, then leaves for a short period of time, and the dog disappears. But the trucker scam doesn't fit. You said that the guy who called John knew about the nick in Emily's ear. If it didn't show on the reward flier, then he must have actually seen the dog or gotten the information from someone who did." The cards grew quiet in Cady's hands. "Unless that's how they're financing the operation."

Erin started playing with a pair of dice. "That's cold-blooded. Steal the dogs for research or whatever, then con the heartbroken owners out of what they were willing to give as a reward so you can feed and house the dogs until you bunch them."

The hair on the back of Lyric's arms was practically dancing. "I'll need to follow up with the other owners, see how many of them paid out or at least were contacted."

Erin dropped the pair of dice on the table. Double sixes. "I'm at loose ends right now, I can make those calls for you."

"I'll spread the newspaper archive search to a wider area," Cady said, "and keep working the rescue angle if you want."

Lyric smiled, grateful for their help. "Hey, I appreciate that."

Cady shuffled the cards, weaving them through her fingers in an intricate pattern. "It'll cost you though. One game, Five Card Stud, losers have to share their latest sexual exploit."

Erin rolled her eyes. "Get real—you do *not* want to hear another 'Encounter with The Purple Vibrator' story."

Cady and Lyric both snickered. Lyric said, "Make it Texas Hold'Em and I'm in." At least with that game she had a fifty-fifty chance. Cady was hard to beat at Five Card Stud.

* * * * *

Lyric left Crime Tells and headed to the animal shelter. She had a phone call to make and she definitely didn't want her sisters to overhear her. Lyric grimaced—there would be hell to pay if they had any clue what she was thinking of doing—but, she couldn't help herself. This was just how she operated.

And why you need a man like Kieran—to keep you from going over the line.

She nearly slammed on the brakes. Shit—where had that come from? Rough, wild sex did *not* make for a controlling interest in her non-bedroom behavior!

Lyric pulled into a shopping center parking lot and dug out her cell phone. When Erin had found the newspaper story about the dog stolen while its owner bought candy, Lyric had immediately recognized the *Tribune* reporter's byline. Celine VanDenbergh.

She'd run across the name. A lot.

Celine had covered the great "clock-tower" protest in Berkeley when members of the Animal Freedom Front had climbed the historic tower and tied themselves to its face in order to protest the use of animals in laboratory testing. She'd also been on the story when the Animal Freedom Front, the AFF, broke into an underground biomedical research facility and liberated a large number of beagles, trashing the place in the process, which, given the security at Gene Masters, should have been impossible.

Celine's stories were always factual, but she usually managed to tilt them in favor of the AFF. With the Gene Masters story, she'd worked in the fact that while some research institutions allow "retired" animals to be released to rescue groups or adopted by citizens, the scientist in charge of the Gene Masters beagles had a "no-release" policy because if scientists knew the animals had a chance of making it out alive, then they might hesitate to perform experiments on them. The AFF members responsible had never been identified or caught, while the editorials generated by her story had been full of angry protests directed at the scientist.

There were other stories and articles that Lyric had run across in magazines, some of which contained interviews or comments from AFF members—not an easy accomplishment with an extremist group that operated so far underground that the FBI couldn't find them. Lyric was praying that she wouldn't need to find the AFF either, that somehow she'd be able to retrieve Anna and John's... She grimaced. Who was she kidding? She hoped she could retrieve *all* of the missing dogs before they got as far as an auction, but if she couldn't then she needed to set some wheels in motion—and her sixth sense told her that a call to Celine VanDenbergh was the way to do it.

Lyric dialed the *Tribune* and got through to the reporter. Celine's voice was surprisingly soft. Somehow Lyric had expected an edgy, hard-bitten reporter-type. She introduced herself and gave a brief summary of the case— emphasizing the number of dogs missing.

"Can you send me a copy of Rickard's photo?" Celine asked. "I can show it to the boy and the convenience store clerk, maybe they can make an identification."

"Sure." Lyric hesitated a heartbeat, trying for the right balance of bait and hook. "You cover a lot of animal welfare stories. Are you interested in an exclusive? With photos and details that will expose how horrible bunching and selling dogs is?"

"What do you have in mind?"

"We pass information to each other to start with."

Celine didn't answer immediately. Lyric hadn't expected her to—not if she was right about the true nature of Celine's involvement with the AFF. The reporter hadn't operated this long out in the open by being trusting. Finally Celine said, "We can try it. What's your next move?"

Satisfaction raced through Lyric. It was just a small tug on her line, but it was enough for now. "I'm heading to animal control. I've got an in with someone who works there. I'm going to see if she's heard any rumors about a sale, or had any complaints that might lead to the dogs."

"That's a good move. How can I reach you?"

Lyric gave the reporter her phone numbers and got a cell number and e-mail address in return. "I'll send you the picture as soon as I can."

"I'll start asking around."

Lyric was still mulling over the conversation with Celine when she got to the animal shelter. Luckily it was late enough in the day that the intake desk was quiet. She stopped by the lost-and-found counter and checked through index cards that served as a file. There were no dachshunds listed in the "found" file. She added Anna's dogs to the "lost file" and compared the other lost animals to the list she'd compiled. No new dogs missing—yet.

She moved on to Tracy's office—a tiny, windowless prison that was cluttered with papers. The shelter supervisor looked up from her phone call and gave a little wave. Lyric moved a pile of papers off one chair and onto another so she could sit.

A rabbit cage, complete with dwarf occupant, took up one corner of the room. A rat was curled up in its cage on the bookshelf behind Tracy's desk. A hamster slept on its wheel in the cage on Tracy's desk. Lyric knew that an ancient Golden Retriever was stretched out on a pile of blankets behind Tracy's chair.

The receiver dropped into its cradle. "You don't want a boa constrictor, do you?" Tracy asked, opening the hamster cage and pulling the fluffy ball of fur out.

Lyric shook her head. "No thanks."

Tracy shrugged. "Worth a try. What's up?" Lyric told her about the missing dogs and the connection to Rickard. Tracy frowned. "That's a lot of missing dachshunds. All miniatures?"

"Yeah." Lyric handed her copies of the fliers for Anna and John's dogs.

"I'll keep an eye out for them. I'm checking the kennels at least three times each shift these days."

"Have any complaints come in? If someone's bunching them, they'll need a place to keep them."

"I haven't heard anything lately that might help. But I'll start checking around with the animal control officers. It's possible that one of them has been out on a complaint for noise or odor. A guy like Rickard wouldn't waste any time or money on caring for the animals. Throw out some food, maybe, but let the animals stay in their own feces and urine until sale time. Why bother cleaning up when you're going to be moving on?"

"So no rumors about an upcoming sale?"

Tracy shook her head. "No. I'll check, but don't hold your breath."

The phone started ringing. Tracy cast a tired glance in its direction and put the hamster back in its cage. Lyric stood. "Call if you hear anything, okay?"

Tracy nodded and reached for her phone. "Will do." She paused, her hand hovering over the phone receiver. "You sure you don't want a boa?"

"I'll ask around for you. How big is it?"

"Little. Three feet, two inches. And absolutely gorgeous if you're into boas. It's an albino, cream-colored background with a contrasting orange pattern. The orange goes from light on the head to dark toward the tail."

* * * * *

Kieran rolled his shoulders. Shit. He'd only meant to stop by the station for a few minutes—just long enough to pass off some case files so those investigations wouldn't stall out while he took time off to deal with his grandmother's dogs. But as soon as he'd hit the bullpen, one thing after another had come up. His mind wandered to Lyric and his cock instantly pulsed. Fuck, he didn't trust the little hellion not to go after Rickard. As soon as he got out of here…

Kieran braced himself as his partner, Cash Sedillo, came in, followed by a bounty hunter named Dasan Nahtailsh. Both men made a beeline straight to Kieran's desk. "Hey, what are doing here?" his partner asked. "I thought you were busy tracking missing dogs. I bet that's a real howl." And like about fifteen guys before him, Cash drew out the word howl in a credible imitation of a dog with its nuts being squeezed.

Cash moved to sit on the edge of Kieran's desk. "I ran into Tyler Keane a little while ago. He said Lyric Montgomery's got your dick tied in a knot, so when I heard you were here, I came up to see for myself." His smile widened. "She's a babe. If you strike out, send her my way. Hell, even if you don't strike out, send her my way. I'd fuck her in a heartbeat."

Before he could control the fury whipping through him, Kieran lunged forward and grabbed the front of Cash's shirt. "Stay the fuck away from her. I'm not sharing." *This one.*

Cash laughed and turned his head slightly. "What do you think, Dasan? Does he look like a man who's got his dick in a twist?"

The bounty hunter's lips tilted up with just the faintest hint of a smile. "Looks that way."

Kieran released the grip on Cash's shirt and sat back down. Son of a bitch! He should have known Cash was baiting him. "I'm trying to get some work done here. Do you think you can take your comedy routine somewhere else?"

Cash grinned. "No problem. We'll just head out and catch some bad guys."

Kieran finished a little while later and left the station. Christ, he felt like a junkie racing on speed. All he could think about was finding Lyric.

Oh yeah, he owed her—for slipping out of his house this morning, for making him lose control in front of his grandmother's house. Fuck. He still couldn't believe that he'd come like some geek teen who jerked off over pictures and shot his load the first time a real babe touched him.

Chapter Eight

Kieran found Lyric at his grandmother's place, which made things a hell of a lot easier than he was expecting them to be. A shared meal, a peck on the cheek afterward, a claim that he and Lyric needed to discuss the case, and he had her out of his grandmother's house and into his. Kieran had never been so glad that he lived near his grandmother.

"I'm still pissed about your sneaking home this morning," he said as soon as he got her inside.

The little hellion had the nerve to laugh, to wrap her arms around his neck, teasing him by pressing her lips against his, by rubbing her pelvis against his. "What can I do to make it up to you?" She slipped her tongue into his mouth, twining it with his, dueling with him for control.

He let her play, let her tease, turned on by the way she liked to push the limits, by the way she challenged him to tame her. Every encounter was like starting over again with her, a fresh show of fiery independence that had the blood rushing to his cock and the urge to dominate sizzling along every nerve ending.

His body tightened in anticipation as he unzipped his pants and freed his cock. "You want to make it up to me, baby, then put your mouth on me, show me how sorry you are for leaving my bed this morning."

Without a word she slid down his body, but rather than take him in her mouth, she licked across the head of his penis, then slowly ran her tongue over his shaft, covering each flushed inch of him while his cock jumped and pulsed under the wet lashes of her tongue.

He groaned and buried his fingers in her hair, holding her against him as his buttocks tightened and clenched. "Suck it!" he growled, knowing she'd do what she damned well pleased but unable to keep himself from issuing the order.

Lyric's husky laugh sent shivers up his spine. The feel of her fingers, cupping and squeezing, exploring his tight balls and the smooth skin behind them, made him hunch over. Son of a bitch, one more second and he was going to wrench her mouth open and shove himself inside.

Her tongue flicked over the head, exploring the leaking slit, sending fire right up his shaft. He groaned, in agony, in ecstasy—he couldn't tell the difference anymore. All he knew was that he was going to die if she didn't suck him, didn't let him fuck in and out of her hot, wet mouth.

"God, Lyric!" It came out a demand, a plea, and then he was beyond all rational thought as she began sucking. In some part of his mind, he tried to hold back, but she didn't let him. She drove him to the edge with her fingers, her mouth, the moans she made as she brought him to an orgasm that left him dizzy. And even then, she continued to torment him, to suck and soothe, and only slowly let him escape the heaven of her mouth.

Kieran's ears were still ringing as he looked down and caught the little hellion's smile. Son of a bitch. He'd never experienced anything like that before. Lyric slowly rose, cuddling against him and burying her face in his neck. He could feel her smile against his skin. "Apology accepted?"

Oh yeah. But damned if he'd let her know that. "Not yet, baby." Not until he'd made her as helpless as she'd just made him.

He led her to the bedroom, taking off his shirt and shoes but nothing else before ordering, "You know what I want, Lyric. Strip."

Defiance flashed in her eyes and his smile became feral. He'd been counting on that. "Strip, baby, or I'm going to rip your clothes off you. That'd be one way to make sure you don't sneak out again."

She slowly peeled out of her clothing, touching herself, teasing him—doing everything she could to send all the blood in his body straight to his cock. He'd been counting on that, too.

"You want to tease, baby? Well, two can play at that." He moved over to the dresser and pulled out a soft, thin, strip of leather, satisfaction whipping through him at the way her eyes widened, at the way she couldn't seem to take her eyes off the binding in his hands as he walked toward her.

At the last minute, she tried to escape, but it was too late by then. He tumbled her to the bed and made short work of lashing her wrists together.

Excitement and fear warred inside of Lyric. She'd never trusted any man enough to let him render her completely helpless. Sure, she'd played some bondage games, but always with ties that were easily broken—a symbol and not a reality.

Kieran's lips covered hers, his tongue savage and demanding as it thrust in and out of her mouth. Her heart was thundering in her ears, racing in her chest when the kiss ended and he pulled her to her knees, turning her so that she faced the headboard, and securing her hands to the rigid frame.

His hand landed sharply on her bare buttocks. "Spread your knees." When she didn't obey immediately, he slapped her ass again, sending a stinging burst of pleasure through her nipples and clit.

She spread her knees and was immediately rewarded by his fingers sliding along the swollen lips of her sex, smearing her juices over her engorged clit. "Baby, you're so responsive. I love the feel of all this smooth flesh," he whispered against her neck, petting her mound before circling her clit, stroking it until she cried out, trying to close her legs against the sharp need whipping through her pussy. He slapped her buttock again. "Oh no, Lyric, you wanted to tease and I told you that two could play that game. Now it's my turn."

His mouth sucked at her neck and shoulders while his fingers tormented her nipples and clit. Any effort to evade his touch, to end his sensual torment led to the sharp, erotic sting of his hand across her buttocks. He teased until Lyric began begging and pleading, humping into his hand, desperate for the orgasm he kept just out of her reach.

Kieran he knew he wasn't going to last, but he didn't care. The moment he'd stuck his hand in her panties and discovered her bare cunt, he'd been fantasizing about this, about tying her to his bed and having her ride his face while he fucked her with his tongue.

Groaning, Kieran pulled away, sliding between her legs even as she whimpered in protest at the loss of this hand. He grabbed her hips and held her in position, ready to demand that she give him what he wanted, but at the first stroke of his tongue, she sobbed and began rubbing against him, filling his world with the sight and smell and pleasure of her swollen, wet pussy.

Kieran ate her up, claimed her in a way that he'd never claimed another woman, and when she came, screaming and thrashing above him, her orgasm triggered his own and sent hot jets of semen over his abdomen, over her buttocks.

Even then, Kieran knew he wasn't finished with her. He moved from the bed, releasing her wrists, frowning at the red marks her wild thrashing had left, but before he could say anything, the little hellion laughed. "Let's take a shower, then we can do it all over again. Except this time, you get to be tied to the bed."

His cock twitched in response. Son of a bitch. She was addictive. "I don't think so, baby," he said as he led her to the shower. She was way too tricky to be trusted. Fuck, his control was already nonexistent around her. If she knew how much time he spent thinking about her, wanting her, needing her… But maybe one day… His cock jerked again at the thought of being at her mercy. Goddamn, where had that come from?

* * * * *

The phone call came as Lyric was just waking up to the feel of Kieran's warm arm around her waist, his hand tucked between her legs, cupping her mound, his morning-hard cock pressed against her buttocks. She thought about letting the call go to voice mail, and probably would have if her jeans hadn't been on the floor right next to the bed. She snagged them and fished out the phone, coming completely alert when she saw who was calling. Tracy.

"You've got something?" Lyric said, aware that Kieran was fully awake now and listening.

"One of your missing dogs was just picked up. I got the call a minute ago and headed them off before they could call the owner. The AC officer took him to the emergency clinic over on Bascom. He's been hit by a car. I figured it'd be easier if you broke the news and helped the owner through this."

"It's one of Anna Simmons' dogs?"

"Yeah, they have a microchip reader at the clinic. It came up with her information."

"How bad is he hurt?"

"I don't know. I called the clinic but they were busy with a lot of other emergencies and didn't have time to give me any details."

"I owe you."

Tracy laughed. "About that boa…"

"Okay. But only on the condition that it's temporary, until I can find it a good home."

"One boa—just adopted. Pick it up sooner rather than later if you don't mind. And don't worry about buying supplies. It comes complete with everything you need, except mice to feed it—you've got to deal with that on you own."

"Where'd the thing come from anyway?"

"The cops. Some bozo drug dealer had a collection of them. He thought he could hide his stash in their cages and it'd be safe there. This is the only one we have left— and believe me, you do not want to know how many of the dealer's friends and clients have come around and tried to get these snakes."

Lyric felt Kieran's presence at her back and smiled as a thought took hold. Somehow it seemed fair that a vice cop should end up with the snake. She thanked Tracy again and hung up, the momentary flash of humor over the snake gone as she and Kieran both climbed out of bed. "You heard?"

Kieran's face was tight. "Enough. I don't want to tell Grandma until I know how bad it is."

Lyric started to object but he pulled her against his body, covering her mouth with his. Underneath the fierce kiss, she could feel the tight knot of fear and concern for his grandmother. "Just hold off calling until we know more, okay?" he said when he released her.

She pressed her lips to his in gentle understanding. "Okay."

* * * * *

The dachshund was lying on a towel in one of the metal cages. Two of his legs were bandaged, and there was a long sutured gash on top of his head. The hair on both his shoulder and hip had been rubbed off when he'd slid across the asphalt of the road. Only the steady rise and fall of his chest confirmed that he was asleep and not dead.

A white-coated veterinarian made his way over and introduced himself with a Texas accent. "This little guy sure got himself banged up."

"Is he going to make it?" Kieran asked.

"Well, I think he's going to do just fine. Right now he's doped up. One of his legs is broken. He'll probably need some orthopedic surgery. But overall, I'd say he's lucky. A cut on the head, but no injury to the skull. And his back is all right. I always worry about these low, long-backed fellas."

"When will the drugs start to wear off?" Lyric asked.

"Another three hours or so. He'll need to be moved to his regular veterinarian, they may want to keep him under observation for a while before sending him home."

Kieran turned to Lyric. "Do you know who Grandma's vet is?"

Lyric mentally ran through her notes. "No. I can call her—or you can. There's no reason not to now that we know Max is going to pull through."

A muscle twitched in Kieran's cheek, but finally he nodded. "You call her. I'll go pay the bill. I don't want her driving while she's upset. Tell her we'll swing by and pick her up."

The veterinarian smiled. "Good. I'll have one of my staff members get the paperwork ready."

It took some maneuvering for Lyric to get away from Kieran, but she managed it, primarily because he wanted to stay close to his grandmother, and also because she told him that she had to make good on her promise to Tracy. She did, collecting the snake and settling it in at Kieran's house even as her mind raced with possibilities.

Her sixth sense was screaming and there was no way she was going to let the trail go cold. Either Harry Rickard had finally figured out that Max was neutered, and dumped him, or the dog had escaped. Lyric was betting on the second scenario—and thanks to the records the emergency vet clinic had, she knew exactly where Max had been picked up.

Now the search could begin in earnest. She opened her cellular and dialed Crime Tells.

Cady answered right away. "Hey, perfect timing. Erin and I were just talking about calling you. We've been following up on those other missing dogs and get this, a black van was spotted in the area two times, a red Corvette was seen five times. Didn't John Merriman say he'd seen a red Corvette the day his dog disappeared?"

Excitement raced through Lyric. They were getting somewhere! "Yeah, he did. Look, I've had another break in the case down here." She told them about Max's recovery and her plan to start doing a search of the area where he'd been found. "If I locate the house where the dogs are, I'll need something besides the Jeep to haul the dogs in."

"You need one us to help you," Cady said. Since she and Erin both had horses and horse trailers, they both had trucks. She grimaced. This was not a job for Erin. Despite the fact that Erin wasn't a cop any more, she had a harder time looking the other way when Lyric did what Lyric was going to do. "Why don't I meet up with you? Maybe Erin can go talk to John Merriman's neighbors. If someone saw the Corvette, it could be another break. I doubt the hired help is driving that car."

Lyric's laugh said she knew exactly what Cady had been thinking. "Good plan. I'll call ahead and talk to John. I'm sure he'll want to help Erin. See you in a few."

"On my way."

* * * * *

Erin could see why Lyric liked John Merriman. Five seconds after meeting him, Erin was just as committed to getting his dog back as Lyric was.

Her heart did a little skip in her chest as her thoughts turned to Lyric and Cady. Though Cady hadn't said exactly what she and Lyric were going to be doing, Erin knew her youngest sister well enough to guess, and pray. *God, please don't let them run into Harry Rickard. Let them find the dogs and get them out safely, but don't let them find him!*

Erin resolutely pushed as much of her worry aside as she could in order to concentrate on what she was doing. She turned to John. "If you're ready, let's go talk to your neighbors. I can do a rough sketch if one of them saw the car and can describe the driver, but I'm a little rusty. If I can't get close enough to the likeness, then we've got an in with a police artist."

John chuckled. "I assume you mean Tyler." When Erin raised a surprised eyebrow, he added, "I'm not sure Anna's grandson would approve of him helping out again."

Part of Erin knew she shouldn't pry, but what the hell, that's what good sisters did — and a small payback for all the worry that Lyric's antics generated. "So you've met the vice cop?"

John chuckled again. "Yes, briefly. Anna assures me that I saw Kieran at his worst. He wasn't very happy about Tyler kissing your sister."

Erin grinned. Oh yeah, she could just see that. What guy wouldn't be jealous as hell of Tyler? Tyler was a walking fantasy.

"Tyler grew up with us. He's almost like a brother."

John winked at her. "I'll pass that on to Anna. She was a little concerned. She's hoping for a big wedding and the first of many great-grandchildren."

Surprise left Erin momentarily speechless. Lyric, married to a cop? Oh boy, that'd be something.

Sex with a totally alpha male, yes, but marriage... Erin started to say *no way*, then thought better of it, remembering Lyric's long heartfelt sigh and her whispered admission. *Yeah, I'm in trouble – big trouble.* Erin shook her head to clear it and followed John across the street.

* * * * *

"Oh my, yes. I remember that car." Doris patted blue-gray hair with one hand and looked in the direction of her husband. "In fact, I pointed it out to Arthur. Didn't I, dear?"

Arthur only had time to nod before she said, "Such a strange-looking young man driving it. Poor thing. Must not tan. I remember saying that to Arthur. He has a cousin that's the same way. White as a sheet all year 'round. And he's a redhead, so he gets those terrible freckles. Doesn't he, dear?"

Erin couldn't stop herself from glancing at Arthur again. He nodded but didn't look up from the television. "Was the man driving the Corvette a redhead, too?"

"Oh no. Pale, pale blond hair, almost white." She shuddered. "He pulled up in front of the house. At first I thought he was a salesman. So I told Arthur to get ready. We're on a fixed income, you know. And over the years we've learned not to let salesmen in. Poor Arthur, he always gets the job of shooing them away. Don't you, dear?" This time Arthur made no move to reply.

"Did he get out of the car?" Erin asked. "Did you get a good look at his face?"

"No. He opened his glove box and pulled out a map. Then he studied it for a long time before he drove away."

"Did you see him again?"

"Not him. But we saw the car again. It was parked down the street. Of course, we didn't know if it was the same car or not. I pointed it out to Arthur. Didn't I, dear?"

Erin turned her attention to Arthur. "Is there anything you can add?"

"What?" he said.

"Is there anything you can add?"

His wife frowned, then yelled, "Turn up your hearing aid."

Arthur did as ordered. Erin asked, "Did you get a good look at the man driving the Corvette?"

He looked puzzled by the question. "What Corvette? What color was it? I don't remember seeing a car like that around here."

Erin wanted to scream, or at least rub her head before it exploded with frustration. She didn't know whether to believe Doris' story or not. As soon as they stepped out of the house, she asked John.

"Doris doesn't miss a thing. She saw him all right."

Unfortunately, she was the only neighbor who did. And she hadn't gotten a good enough view for a sketch.

* * * * *

Cady looked at the slightly irregular rectangle that was traced on the map that rested on the seat between her and Lyric. "This is the search area?"

"Yeah. You can see here that these two sides are bordered by highway. This side is bordered by the river, and this one by business areas. If Max got out of someone's backyard, I think he'd end up somewhere within this outlined area."

"The X is where he was found?"

"Yeah. I've already covered it on foot. The dogs would have stuck together, at least until Max got hit. I think the girls would still be together, but so far nothing, and no one's seen them."

"So maybe only Max got out."

"Maybe." Lyric tapped the left side of the rectangle. "I'll start at this end, you start at the other, we'll cover more ground that way." She handed Cady the picture that Tyler had done of Harry Rickard. "Be careful, okay?"

Cady rolled her eyes. "Oh that's rich, coming from you." She made a show of looking around. "So where's the cop? And better yet, does he have a clue what you're doing?"

Heat flushed through Lyric's face. But a shiver pulsed down her spine and through her clit. *Rule number two — I'm in charge of this case. If I say stay away from parts of it, you better keep the fuck away.* "Let's not worry about him now. Ready?"

Cady nodded. "Meet you in the middle somewhere."

* * * * *

An hour later Cady stopped to get a cold drink. The girl working behind the counter looked barely sixteen. Her shirt captured Cady's attention with its picture of a Chihuahua sitting in a teacup with a caption that read — *Wonderful things come in small packages.*

"Great shirt! Are you crazy about dogs, or do you just like the saying?"

The girl laughed. "Oh, I'm crazy about dogs. One day I want to be a veterinarian."

Cady smiled. "Working around animals is a lot of fun. I do pet portraits."

"For real? People pay you to paint pictures of their animals?"

"Take photographs."

"Cool."

Cady twisted the top off of her drink. "My sister is a detective who specializes in finding missing pets."

The girl leaned against the counter. "No way!"

Cady laughed. "Yeah. Today I'm helping her. Last night one of the dogs she's looking for was found nearby. He was hit by a car."

"That sucks! Is he going to live?"

"Yeah. But there might have been two other dogs with him—all three of them were stolen."

"No shit?"

Cady grinned. "No shit. All three dogs are miniature dachshunds. Have you seen any loose dogs?"

"No. I've worked almost every day this week, but I haven't seen any stray dogs at all."

Cady pulled out the picture of Rickard. Recognition flashed across the girl's features. "Hey, he comes by every couple of days for beer and cigarettes." Her eyes widened. "You think he stole them?"

"Yep. Does he come by at a particular time?"

The girl shook her head. "Not that I've noticed. Let me ask Paulo if he knows." She stepped away from the cash register and stuck her head through a doorway that led to the stockroom. "Paulo, can you come out here for a minute?"

A tall, lanky teenager strolled out. "What do you want?"

She handed him the picture. "You've seen this guy, right?"

Paulo squinted first at the picture, then at Cady. "Why do you want to know?"

Before Cady could answer, the girl said, "She thinks he stole some dogs." Some of the interest left the boy's face. "Well?" the girl demanded.

He shrugged. "I think he lives over on Fulton."

Cady held her hand out for the picture. "Thanks."

"Just don't say you heard it from me."

Paulo started to turn away and Cady said, "Look, if you see him, be careful, okay. And try to call the cops." Both teens froze. Cady bit her lip, then figured—what the hell—she couldn't walk away and wonder if the next convenience store Rickard robbed, and the next people he shot would be these two. She put the picture on the counter. "This guy escaped from Lompoc Penitentiary. He was in for armed robbery, shot two people while he was robbing a store like this one."

"Holy shit!" the boy breathed.

"For real?" the girl asked.

"For real. So show this to the other people who work here and be careful. Okay?"

* * * * *

Fulton Avenue was a relatively short street, maybe forty houses, twenty on each side, none of which had a black van parked in front of it. "Door to door?" Cady asked from the passenger seat of Lyric's Jeep.

Lyric studied the street in front of them. "Let's drive down and back one time first."

At the end of the street, Cady said, "Hold on. I think I see something," and Lyric eased the Jeep over to the curb in front of a run-down house.

The front yard was bare dirt littered with newspapers and other household junk. A refrigerator lay on its side, its door several yards away holding up a rapidly deteriorating fence. Through a hole in the fence they could see a dog run in the backyard, but the grass was knee-high, so there was no way to see if there were dogs in the run or not.

"I don't hear any barking," Lyric said, but her sixth sense was humming. "Stay here while I check it out." When Cady opened her mouth to protest, Lyric shook her head. "I need you for backup. Keep your cell out."

Lyric got out of the car and walked to the front door. She was willing to play the odds. There wasn't any reason for Rickard to recognize her and her gut told her he wasn't home. The house had a quiet feel to it. She knocked, loudly enough to get a dog barking.

Nothing.

Shooting a "stay put" look toward the Jeep, Lyric moved around the side of the house, careful to negotiate through the broken glass and rusted junk. A gate to the backyard hung partway opened, held up by the ground and one rusted hinge. Lyric eased around it and followed a well-worn path to the dog run.

The dachshunds had been there—more than just three of them. The urine and feces testified to that—along with the bag of dog food thrown in the center of the run, a long slash ripped down its center to allow the dogs to get at its contents. There was still plenty of food left. In another day or so, the birds, raccoons and rats would have it taken care of.

Lyric kicked a rusty coffee can and sent it sailing into the chain-link fence. Her stomach churned with rage while her heart screamed with worry. Shit!

She wouldn't risk Erin or Cady by asking them to stake out Rickard's house on the long shot that he was coming back. And she couldn't waste time waiting for it to get dark so she could break in and see if he left a trail. She went back to the Jeep and called Kieran.

Chapter Nine

Kieran eyed the snake that had taken up residence in his TV room. He'd like to think it was a sign that Lyric planned on spending a lot of time at his house, in his bed—kind of her version of moving in some extra clothes and a toothbrush.

Not a fucking chance.

She was a lot trickier than that. This wasn't anything except her attempt to saddle him with a pet. Knowing her, she probably thought he had it coming to him.

Son of a bitch, she was fun to try and outguess and outsmart. Until she'd come into his life, brains hadn't exactly been high on his list when it came to female companionship. Decent looks and spread legs had pretty much done it for him.

Shit, she'd ruined him for that, just like she'd ruined him for anything but a smooth pussy. His cock tightened and pulsed just thinking about that part of her anatomy. The truth was, she'd ruined him for anyone but her. She'd turned him into a fucking addict—and he couldn't even stay pissed about it.

Heaven was tunneling into her tight little cunt, sucking her breasts and hearing her whimper and scream while he showed her who was in charge. Hell would be doing without her—and he didn't plan of visiting Hell anytime soon.

Kieran moved away from the snake and made his phone call. He hated owing someone—and owing a bounty hunter could lead to a shitload of trouble with the captain—but this thing with the dogs needed to be wrapped up. He hated what it was doing to his grandmother, and he hated the constant gnawing in his gut that Lyric was going to meet up with Rickard and get hurt...or worse.

He stalked back to glower at the snake. Speaking of Lyric, just where the fuck was she? Goddamn, he was going to tag her with a tracking unit if she didn't... His cell rang, interrupting the rant. His cock jerked when he saw it was Lyric calling.

"Baby, I'm pretty pissed right now. I expected to find you at your place or here—instead, all I'm finding is a snake."

Silence greeted his statement. Then the little hellion had the nerve to laugh and say, "You want me to call back later?"

"I want you to tell me where you are and what you've been doing."

"I found Rickard's place. It looks like he bolted."

Fear ripped through Kieran's gut. "Fuck! You did what?" He listened to her answer with a death grip on the cellular.

She ended with, "I figured you'd know who to pass the information along to, maybe suggest a search to see if he left a trail."

The blood was pounding so loudly in Kieran's head that he was surprised he could hear, let alone think. When he got his hands on her... "Just what part of Rule Number

Two didn't you understand? I told you to stay the fuck away from Rickard!"

There was a moment of silence. "Does this mean you're going to punish me?"

His cock went so hard, so fast that it was all Kieran could do to stand up straight. He unzipped his pants and freed his penis in an effort to relieve some of the pressure, but the feel of skin-on-skin, even if it was his own, only made it worse. Son of a bitch, the little hellion was still trying to control the situation—she knew how her words would affect him. Well, he'd give her what she was asking for. "Yeah, baby, I think you can pretty much count on being punished."

Lyric laughed and his hand tightened involuntarily on his cock as a wave of searing heat ran through it. "I'll see you later then," she said and the line went dead.

* * * * *

To distract herself from the ache between her legs, and keep herself from racing to Kieran's house, Lyric checked her voice mail. Caroline from dachshund rescue had called. Lyric called her back.

"You might have already talked to these people, but I wanted to be sure," Caroline said. "They found a female dachshund about a week ago and put an ad in the newspaper. This morning a man called and claimed the dog. The dog didn't seem to recognize him, but they felt helpless to stop him from leaving with her. They were very distressed and called me. I didn't have the heart to tell them that this is one way bunchers acquire animals."

"Do you have their number?"

Caroline laughed. "Right next to the phone for a change. Their names are Maggie and Walter Jacobson, delightful people — elderly. I'd love to place a dog with them."

Lyric caught the Jacobsons at home. "I should never have let him leave with Angel," Maggie said. "He was so friendly over the phone. But when he came to the house, I didn't feel right about him. And Angel didn't seem to recognize him. She's been so friendly with everyone who's come to visit. It wasn't like her to keep her distance. We fell in love with her — that's the reason we put the ad in the newspaper. Walter and I thought someone else might be hurting over losing her, but I guess we were hoping that her owner wouldn't claim her. She's so easy to love, and so much fun to have around. Angel gave us a reason to go for walks again, and we've met so many friendly people. Why she's even been sleeping with us. She burrows down under the covers then comes back up and sleeps with her head on the pillow between us. I asked Tony if he was sure that she was his dog, and he said yes."

"Did you get a last name?" Not that there was any guarantee that Tony was his real name.

"No, he may have mentioned it over the phone, but I was… I felt heartsick when he called."

"Can you describe him?"

Maggie sighed. "I'm ashamed to admit this. Maybe the reason I didn't feel comfortable letting Angel go was because Tony was so strange-looking. It was a bit unnerving — though I know it's not nice to say those things these days."

Lyric willed Maggie to describe the same man that John's neighbor had described to Erin. "What do you mean strange-looking?"

"Very pale, almost albino except that he had blue eyes—light, light blue eyes." Maggie sighed again. "After talking to Caroline, I realize now that I should have made Tony show me some proof that Angel was his. I guess that's why I took down his license plate number. The house has been lonely without Angel."

Excitement ripped through Lyric. "What kind of car was Tony driving?"

"A truck. One of those small trucks, with a shell on the back."

"What color was it?"

"White."

"Do you remember the make?"

"No, I'm afraid I didn't notice. Is it important?" Then before Lyric could answer Maggie's question, she added in an alarmed voice, "Do you think he lied about Angel belonging to him?"

"I'm not sure," Lyric said, sparing them from the truth. "Let me have the license number. I'll do some checking."

Maggie read off the number. "Can you get our Angel back?"

"I'll do what I can."

"Is it all right if we call?"

"That would be fine," Lyric said and got a description of the dog before hanging up.

Lyric studied the license plate number and contemplated her next move. The easiest thing to do would be to give it to Kieran and have him run a DMV check, but that could get messy, especially if there were…repercussions…from what she did with the information. Calling Tyler was out for the same reason. He'd have trouble coming up with an alibi—not that he couldn't, but digging into the DMV records wasn't exactly an everyday need for a police artist. She needed the information fast and that left one other obvious choice. Celine VanDenbergh.

"I've got a license plate number. Do you have any sources that can run it?"

"California?"

"Yes."

"What is it?"

Lyric read off the number. "White truck, compact."

"A buncher?"

"Yeah. Seen at least one other time when a dog went missing. This time he showed up claiming he was the owner of a 'found' dog."

"I'll call you back."

It took less than ten minutes for Celine to get back with an answer. "Good catch. The car's registered to Bio-Specimens. They're in LA. I assume you want the address?"

"Yeah."

Celine rattled it off. "You're going to check it out?"

"As soon as I can get to the airport and get a ticket."

"You'll tell me what you find?"

"Sure, I'll e-mail you from the airport."

* * * * *

Kieran wasn't surprised to see Cash show up with Dasan. Just as well he didn't have any secrets from his partner, and if Cash was willing to help, well, it'd get done a lot sooner. Hell, the truth of the matter was that Kieran missed being on the job—working the angles and taking down the bad guys.

Cash made a beeline for the snake's habitat as soon as they walked into the TV room. "Hey, nice snake. Giving the ladies something to compare to when they see what you're packing?"

Kieran eyed the boa as it stretched out on a three-foot branch. "Not even close. What I've got makes him look like a pencil."

Cash grinned. "So this is your new pick-up line? Come home with me, sugar, and I'll show you my snake?" He turned away from the boa's habitat. "But then, maybe you don't need to work the ladies anymore. This Lyric's doing?"

Kieran frowned. He didn't like the casual way her name rolled off his partner's lips. "How do you know her?"

"I don't. Saw her once with Braden, that's all." Cash threw up his hands. "Hey, she's all yours. I haven't met a woman yet who's worth the kind of trouble she is. You know what I like—fast, fuckable, and forgettable—in that order."

The bounty hunter shook his head. "One day you're going to eat those words, my friend. And I'll be there to see it."

Cash laughed. "Forget the prophecy shtick, Nahtailsh, stay with bounty hunting." When Kieran's eyebrows rose in question, Cash said, "Dasan's great, great grandfather was some kind of a shaman—used to dance with rattlers, have visions of the future, the works. Sometimes Dasan can't help himself. He falls back on the old ways and blathers on and on, making ominous predictions—usually about my life."

Kieran shook his head in disbelief. He couldn't picture it. Hell, he'd already heard more words today from the bounty hunter then he'd heard when they were on an eight-hour stakeout together.

Cash moved over to the couch and plopped down. "So what've you got on Harry Rickard? Where do you want to start looking for him?"

Dasan lingered in front of the boa's habitat, accepting that his life was about to change. How it would change, he didn't know, but it would involve the Montgomerys. The snake in Kieran's TV room was an omen sent from his own spirit-guide, a rattlesnake that had shown itself to him when he reached puberty and went on his vision quest—a totem he shared with his father and his father's father, all the way back to the first Nahtailsh shaman.

As Dasan studied the white snake with its orange pattern, he recognized it as the one that had appeared in his dream on the day Rickard had assaulted Kieran's grandmother. He hadn't known then that they were connected, but later, when Cash told him, and then when he heard that a Montgomery was involved, he began suspecting. And now the snake was here—a marker that his life would change. A sign that only a blind man would choose to ignore. He turned from the snake and joined Cash and Kieran.

"If we get a neighbor to identify Rickard's picture, that'll give us probable cause to go in," Kieran was saying.

"Rickard's not the kind of suspect we're usually after," Cash said. "The captain's going to know it's personal. He's not going to like it—especially if we go in without anyone who's got jurisdiction."

Kieran shook his head. "I don't want to open this up. Next thing you know, we'll be locked out of the scene. After we've checked it out, we can call it in."

"Risky."

"I don't give a shit."

"You will when you get put on desk duty or end up directing traffic and checking parking meters."

"I'll go in," Dasan said. "Rickard's wanted. There's reward money on him."

Kieran and Cash exchanged glances. Kieran said, "Fine. Lyric says she thinks Rickard's bolted. The dogs are gone."

Dasan nodded. "Guy like him hasn't survived on his brains. Usually just tries to stay one step ahead of the law. Once I'm in the house, I'll see what he's left that'll lead us to him."

* * * * *

The address Celine provided was in an old, grime-coated industrial section with barred windows over jagged, broken glass. Trash fluttered on the ground with every hot breath of big-city air. Urine and feces contaminated water poured out of a drain at the side of the building and traveled a few feet before heading into the city's sewage system.

Lyric rang the buzzer, each hit ratcheting up the sound of dogs barking inside. Each minute of waiting almost overwhelming her with the stench coming from Bio-Specimens.

A drug-thin, blond man with greasy hair and a speed-jittery body finally opened the door and Lyric said, "I'm looking to buy some dogs. Somebody told me that this was a good place to start."

The blond twitched, his eyes unable to focus on any one spot for long. "The boss doesn't like for people to come around here."

Lyric shrugged. "Well, maybe the guy I was talking to had a few too many. I ran into him in a bar. I'm trying to get a breeding operation going."

"What are you looking for?"

"Dachshunds to start off with. Any color, any age, just so long as they're breedable."

His arms gave a series of tiny jerks. "Can't help you. There's a big order out for them."

"A breeding operation?"

"No, some researcher back east. Heard the boss saying that the guy needs a lot of bodies now — as many as we can come up with."

"So you don't have any dachshunds here at all?"

"No, shipped everything we had this morning."

Lyric's heart tightened into a fist. "They go direct or did they go to the auction." She paused just a second. "I think I heard there was one coming up soon."

"Yeah, Friday and Saturday, somewhere near San Jose."

"You don't know where?"

"No."

"Any way I could talk to your boss and get an invite?"

His body twitched, his eyes focusing on Lyric for a second, long enough for her to see that mentioning his boss had made him afraid. "I've got to get back to work." He hesitated in the doorway. "Look, don't tell anybody you talked to me. The boss doesn't like people knowing her business."

* * * * *

Kieran's guts twisted as he viewed the fetid dog run. Thank God his grandmother would never see this, would never know how terrible it had been for her dogs. Shit, there was a reason he didn't work the gambling rings that ran pit bull fights or cockfights. This kind of stuff crawled under his skin in a way that other situations didn't.

Yeah, he'd seen his fair share of terrible things working vice, but most of the time the humans involved were at least somewhat willing participants—ok, maybe driven to where they were by bad choices they'd made so many years back that they couldn't even remember the day their lives started going down the shithole, but at least at some point, they'd started down the path themselves. But this...

He broke away as Dasan emerged from the house with a plastic garbage bag. "What have you got?"

"Collars. I grabbed them for Lyric."

Tension whipped through Kieran, followed by disgust. Fuck, he felt like one of Pavlov's dogs, going rabid if he thought any other man might have some claim to her. "Anything else?"

"Yeah. You ever heard of a place called Turbo's?"

"Bar downtown. Not known for its stellar clientele."

"That sounds about right. Got matchbooks all over the place from there."

Kieran grinned, feeling victory close by. "Let's go."

They joined Cash at the front of the house. "About time, it was getting pretty boring out here. You're losing your touch, Nahtailsh." Cash made a show of looking at his watch. "Took you seven minutes. A simple B&E plus search like that one, should have taken you four, five max." He eyed the plastic grocery bag now in Kieran's possession. "Where to?"

They headed downtown, Dasan ahead of them in his van, Kieran riding with Cash. "So what's in the bag?" Cash asked.

"Dog collars." Kieran opened the bag, digging through the collars until he found the three he was looking for. "I want a shot at him," he said, thinking about the man who'd hit his grandmother and sent her to the hospital.

"You want me to pull you off before or after you've beat the shit out of him?"

Kieran scowled at his partner. Fuck, sometimes he hated being a cop. He didn't lose any sleep when scum like Rickard got what was coming to them, but if the pounding came from a cop...one hint of police brutality and the liberals and criminal molly-coddlers would be all over his ass, ready to send him to jail.

When he didn't say anything, Cash grinned. "There's always a chance he'll resist arrest."

Kieran's spirits lifted. Yeah. A guy like Rickard didn't know any other way, especially when he was looking at additional prison time for escape and putting a couple of federal guards in the hospital.

They split up when they got to the bar, Cash and Dasan going in through the front, while Kieran came through the back. Rickard was a sitting duck at the bar, one hand on a beer mug, the other fondling a whore who looked like she'd seen more action than a commuter station during rush hour.

He may not have made them as law enforcement, but Rickard had enough street smarts to recognize trouble when he saw it coming his way. He flung the beer mug at Dasan before sweeping his battering ram of an arm into the whore, knocking her to the floor in front of Cash.

Kieran was more than ready for him. He plowed a fist into Rickard's gut and the other man staggered into the bar, immediately scrambling for a bottle to use as a weapon. Kieran didn't give him a chance, another punch had Rickard bending, a third put him on the ground with his arms being wrenched behind his back as all three of them worked to get cuffs on the cursing, bucking felon.

"Where are the dogs?" Kieran growled, his knee riding Rickard's back.

"What dogs? I don't know anything about any fucking dogs."

Rage whipped through Kieran. He wanted to grab the cuffed arms and jerk them back and up, breaking a shoulder if that's what it took.

"Let Dasan transport him," Cash said. "If we don't get him out of here soon, we're going to have company. Then the next time you see him, he'll be all lawyered-up."

It took every bit of willpower Kieran had to stand and step away, to let the bounty hunter pull Rickard to his feet and guide him out of the bar.

"Fuck!"

Cash had the guts to laugh. "Yeah, that's exactly what you need to calm down. Go find Lyric. Give her a reward for the hot tip. Maybe by the time you've finished riding her, Dasan will have convinced Rickard to spill his guts about the dogs."

Kieran's cock went rock-hard at the thought of just what Lyric deserved. *Does this mean you're going to punish me?* Oh yeah, she had something coming all right—for deliberately going against his rules and sneaking off to find Rickard's place.

* * * * *

At least Lyric had the good sense to be waiting for him at his house, to not make him madder by having to hunt her down. He stalked over to where she was standing, apparently fascinated by the internal lump that seemed to be moving toward the tail end of the snake's body. If it was supposed to be symbolic of something, Kieran didn't have the patience to figure it out. "What the fuck were you thinking about going after Rickard!" he yelled, the pent-up fear exploding now that he saw her. "If he'd caught you snooping around his house..." Fuck, he couldn't even go there! The whore Rickard had been fondling when they walked in now had a broken jaw from Rickard knocking her into Cash's path.

The little hellion's eyes flashed fire, which did nothing to calm Kieran down. "Give me some credit here, Kieran. First, I had Cady as backup. Second, I checked the place so I was pretty sure he was gone. And third, I called you when I could have been in and out of there in a heartbeat." She snapped her fingers for emphasis and Kieran saw red.

He reached over and opened her pants, ripping them down her legs before carrying her to the sofa and turning her over his knee. She fought and bucked and wriggled, trying to evade the sharp, punishing slaps to her ass, but he easily restrained her.

Son of a bitch, she'd learn to obey, to leave the dangerous parts of the detective work to him. He was the cop. He was the one who was supposed to take the risks. Period.

Kieran stopped when her ass cheeks were pink and tender. She'd quit struggling by then, though the breath was heaving in and out of her chest, the same as it was doing in his.

His heart thundered as raw emotion threatened to overwhelm him. Christ he couldn't lose her, couldn't stand it if she got hurt.

Kieran smoothed a hand across her buttocks then leaned over, pressing kisses to the sensitive skin before settling her on his lap and rubbing his nose against hers. Her eyes were dazed, shocked, and for once Kieran saw true surrender in them—at least for a small instant in time. He didn't expect it to last, but for the moment, it calmed him.

He took her mouth in a gentle kiss and she responded, cuddling against him. When he lifted his mouth from hers he whispered, "It scared the shit out of me to think of you anywhere near Rickard."

"Did you catch him?"

"Yeah."

Lyric leaned away from him. "He didn't tell you anything?"

"Nothing helpful. Says he got paid in cash, never met the guy in the same place twice and doesn't know what happened to the dogs after he turned them over."

"Dead end."

"Yeah."

Lyric pressed her lips to his, wanting a time-out, wanting to escape the knowledge that they only had one more day before the sale, before it would become almost impossible to recover the dogs. "Make love to me."

Kieran lifted her and carried her to his bedroom.

Chapter Ten

John was at Anna's house the next morning, which caught Kieran off-guard—if the fierce scowl and the "what the fuck's he doing here" were anything to go by when he saw the other man's car parked in front of his grandmother's place. Lyric smiled. She'd seen this one coming from a mile off. Anna and John were perfect company for each other, even if it didn't turn into a romance, though she'd put her money on the table and bet it would.

She stretched, tender and sore but feeling amazingly alive—and well satisfied. If Kieran didn't watch it, his punishments were going to backfire and start her thinking up new ways to misbehave. God, he knew how to turn her on.

When she would have reached for the door handle—Kieran's car for once—he grabbed her wrist and hauled her against his body, his free hand burrowing under her shirt and bra and cupping a sensitive nipple. Lyric couldn't prevent the small whimper from escaping.

Satisfaction flashed through Kieran at the sound. Damn. The day hadn't even started and all he wanted to do was get her back to bed. Son of bitch—she was an obsession he couldn't see his way clear of. "New day, baby, same rules. I'm in charge. Got it?" He tightened his grip on her nipple and watched her pupils expand and contract as pleasure and pain blended. She might submit in the end, but she always fought initially—and that sent a bolt of pure fire to Kieran's cock. *Oh yeah, baby, fight me.* He put more pressure on her nipple and she gave a breathy little whimper that had his cock aching to shove into her and make her scream. "Tell me who's in charge." He ran his tongue along her earlobe, biting down in warning.

Lyric closed her eyes — almost dizzy from the need he generated in her. There was a reason they'd driven over here. It took her a long minute to drag it up — Anna had an idea, something she wanted to try in order to get not just her dogs, but John's Emily, back. Lyric fought through the haze of desire and gave Kieran what he wanted. "You're in charge."

Kieran stroked his tongue into her ear, then nuzzled and bit along her jawbone and neck until his lips moved to whisper above hers, "I know how much you like me to suck your clit and fuck you with my tongue. Behave yourself today and I'll bring you off with my mouth when we get home."

Lyric shivered, swollen, wet and aching for Kieran to take her home and do what he'd just promised…and more. Some part of her knew she should be scared shitless of what she felt for him — but another part screamed that it would die if it didn't get what it needed — what it had to have, what it could get only from him.

She let him help her out of the car and lead her inside, some part of his body always touching hers — as though he craved her with the same intensity. Lyric studied him through half-closed eyes and wondered…until the smell of something baking caused her stomach to ripple and her thoughts to shift from the need burning in her cunt to a simpler hunger.

"Come on into the kitchen and have a seat," John called from the back of the house. "I'm just getting ready to pull some homemade cinnamon rolls out of the oven."

Kieran and Lyric wandered back to the kitchen. John was decked out in an apron bearing a huge green frog with the caption "Kiss the cook!". Anna was hovering next to him.

Donning green mitts that matched the frog on his apron, John pulled the baking sheet out and gently tipped it so the pastries slipped onto a cooling rack. Anna handed him a small plate and he shifted one of the buns to it.

"Have you ever heard of Raphaela King?" Anna asked as she set the plate in front of Lyric, who'd taken John's suggestion and grabbed a seat at the kitchen table.

Lyric frowned. "Raphaela King. The name sounds familiar."

John cleared his throat. "She's an animal communicator."

Kieran snorted. Lyric flicked a glance in his direction. It didn't take a detective — or a cop — to see where this was going. Now she remembered why the name sounded familiar. There'd been an article about Raphaela in one of the dog magazines she subscribed to. "She's up in Sausalito, right?"

Anna nodded and looked over at John, probably for moral support before saying, "Yes, I want to take Max to see her. She's willing to see us this morning."

"Grandma…"

"I'm going to do this, Kieran." She gave Lyric a pleading look. "And I want Lyric to go with us."

A muscle ticced in Kieran's cheek. "Fine, but I'm going, too."

Anna gave a little laugh and patted his hand. "No, I suspect having you there would be like dropping a cone of silence over the gathering. I can't imagine Raphaela would be able to help with you glowering at her like she was a criminal."

Kieran was so startled by his grandmother's comment that he didn't immediately argue. Then by the time he would have opened his mouth, she squeezed his hand and met his look with a determined one of her own. "Please, humor your old grandmother. Lyric will be there to make sure John and I aren't taken advantage of, okay?"

* * * * *

"Look at this," Erin said, pushing her chair back so that Cady could look at the article on the screen.

Valuable Show Dogs Stolen

Show breeder, Mary Jo Rodgers, is stunned by the theft of seven of her show dogs. The dogs were taken from her home while she was at work and include a dog that went Best of Breed in the prestigious Westminster Kennel Club Annual Dog Show. The show, held in Madison Square Garden, is the premier dog show for American dog fanciers.

Police are puzzled by the theft. The burglars entered the house but took only adult dogs. A litter of five puppies was left.

A substantial reward is being offered for any information leading to the recovery of the dogs. A police tip line and the breeder's phone number follow. Anyone having knowledge of this crime is encouraged to call.

Cady tapped the computer screen with the eraser end of her pencil. "It says here that a litter of five puppies was left. If she had puppies, then I'm betting she wasn't taking her dogs out where they might have contact with viruses or germs. Most show breeders are too worried about their puppies coming down with something. So the only way whoever stole the dogs would know about them is if they saw an ad in the paper or followed the show circuit. Either works for me, but I'd bet my money that they answered an ad. I'd also bet that they cased the place first. They wouldn't risk a break-in for just one or two dogs. They must have known it was worth their while to risk it."

Erin nodded. "I'll buy that. All the other dogs have been taken from yards, or gotten free out of the newspaper—except for Anna's dogs and the kid in Oakland. I think those were more crimes of opportunity than premeditated. Plus we know Rickard was responsible for them—and we know that grab and snatch with the possibility of violence is his MO. This feels different—like Tony, the guy in the red Corvette or the white truck."

Cady tapped the computer screen another time. "Yeah. We know he's not afraid of being seen. So far he's the only one who's collected any of the dogs advertised as found." She frowned. "Did you tell Lyric about the calls you made yesterday?"

"Yeah. I left her a voice mail telling her that Tony snagged two dogs last week by pretending he'd lost them." She shrugged. "Unfortunately, both of the people who found the dogs were pretty anxious to get rid of them. They didn't ask for ID or proof that the dogs were his. Kind of a dead end."

Cady sat back in her chair. "We're getting closer on this one, I can feel it."

Erin snickered. "Are you claiming to have the Maguire sixth sense now, like Grandma and Lyric do?"

Cady laughed. "I wish. It'd make my life a lot easier."

"I don't know about that. Have you ever noticed that anyone with the Maguire sixth sense seems to end up in trouble a lot of the time? Look at Braden and Lyric."

Cady thought about it for a minute. "You've got a point there." She directed her gaze to the computer screen. "What next?"

"I think that if they've hit one show breeder, then they'll hit another. Maybe this is our chance to actually get ahead of them. I'll call this breeder first. If we can get an MO, then we can start checking local breeders."

"That's good. Let's go for it!"

Mary Jo Rodgers answered on the third ring. "I'll help any way I can," she said after Erin had introduced herself and told her about the missing dogs in California.

"Great. First question, did you take the dogs for walks or to the local dog park?"

"Good heavens, no! I've got puppies here. I never take the dogs out in public. There are germs everywhere! I can't risk the puppies!"

Erin grinned and gave Cady the thumbs-up. "Were you advertising the puppies?"

"Yes."

"Did you have many responses to the ad?"

Mary Jo made a tsk tsk sound. "Only a few. My puppies don't go cheaply. These puppies were sired by Klaus, you probably know who he is. He went Best of Breed at the Westminster show."

"Did you show the puppies to anyone before the break-in?"

"Yes, I showed them to three different couples. Two of the couples took a puppy home with them. Wonderful people! Of course I've kept in touch with them. They love the puppies."

"What about the third couple?"

"No. They were a nice couple. I wouldn't have shown them the dogs otherwise. They seemed very interested. Knowledgeable. They insisted on seeing the mother and father and any other related adult dogs. She seemed to fall in love with one of the puppies. But her dog just died, and she wasn't sure if she was ready yet. Her boyfriend wanted to buy the puppy on the spot, but I told them to go home and think about it. Of course, I wanted them to have a puppy. But I didn't want them to be impulsive." Mary Jo sighed, "They didn't call. Poor thing, I guess she just isn't ready."

"Did you notice what they were driving?"

"Oh my, yes, a beautiful red Corvette. It sounds horrible to say, but I always check to see what people are driving. I want to make sure they have enough money for vet bills and to provide for their puppies."

"Do you have a phone number or address for this couple?"

"No. Usually I get a phone number. But she couldn't give me one, she was calling from work. Then when they were here, it didn't occur to me. I get that information when I sell a puppy anyway. I like to keep track of them you know."

"Did you happen to notice the license plates on the car?"

Mary Jo was quiet for a moment. "No, no, I didn't. You don't think that couple had anything to do with my dogs disappearing, do you? Surely not, they were lovely people. Why, Leila got tears in her eyes when she talked about her dog. And her boyfriend, I think she called him Tony, was so comforting, so loving."

"What did they look like?"

"Leila was very beautiful. I thought maybe she was a model, but she said no. Dark brown hair, beautiful skin. I think her eyes were brown, too. I'm five-five, so she is probably five-seven. Lovely voice, very charming. Long red nails. Tony was rather odd-looking. I know it's not politically correct to say something like that these days. His skin was very white—at first I though he was albino—but his eyes were a pale, pale blue. The dogs acted funny with him. But he was so loving, so devoted to Leila. I just can't believe they're involved in this."

"Jackpot," Erin whispered to Cady, and if they were really, really lucky, Leila and Tony had visited a local breeder and they could get Tyler to do a quick sketch. If worst came to worst, it was worth a trip to Reno to get a picture.

* * * * *

Raphaela's home was a houseboat. The communicator herself was fiftyish and wore subdued clothing. Lyric had been half-expecting tie-dye. "Come in, come in," she said, opening her arms wide and moving just enough so the dangling crystal earrings swung in a gentle arc.

John kept a steadying hand on Anna's elbow as she moved into the boat with Max in her arms, cradled on a cedar bed to minimize the concussion.

"Have a seat, please, make yourselves comfortable." Raphaela's voice was soft, soothing. Lyric settled in a chair, yielding the couch to John and Anna.

The communicator's living room was decorated in muted pinks and blues. Like the plants under John's care, hers seemed to be thriving, too.

"Can I pour you some tea?" she asked. Only John accepted the offer. She poured both herself and him a cup before asking to hold Max. When Anna hesitated, Raphaela said, "It'll only be for a few moments. I find that the communication is clearer when I can actually touch the animal."

Anna nodded and gently shifted Max onto Raphaela's lap. The little dog wagged his tail. Raphaela placed a hand on Max, then leaned back in her chair—eyes closed.

The room grew very quiet and Lyric's sixth sense started to hum. Max was staring intently at the communicator's face, and the air around them felt…fuller, heavier.

"He's worried about his two companions," Raphaela said in a hushed voice. "They've been together ever since they were puppies and he's always looked after them." Eyes still closed, she stroked the dachshund's head. "He wants you to know that he couldn't do anything to help them. He escaped when the man came into the run with a bag of dog food. There was just a split second to dart through the door."

The hair danced along Lyric's spine as she pictured the dog food bag on the floor of the run. She hadn't shared that with anyone except Erin and Cady. And she doubted Kieran would have described the scene to his grandmother.

Raphael gently rubbed Max's soft ear. "He stayed for a few minutes but the man started chasing him. He tried to come home…but a car hit him." Raphaela shuddered. "He was at the side of the road and the car swerved into him. That's all he remembers until he woke up at the vet's office."

John leaned forward. "Were there other dogs in the run when he got there?"

Raphaela frowned in concentration. "Yes, and even more before those. The run hasn't been cleaned up. Lots of dogs have been there. There are smells from lots of different dogs."

"Did he see Emily there?" John asked, his voice cracking with hope. "She's got a tear in her ear and she loves other dogs."

"Yes. He saw a dog like the one you describe." The communicator gave a shaky sigh and opened her eyes, handing Max back to Anna before reaching for her cup of tea.

Anna's hands shook as she opened her purse and pulled out a picture of all three dogs and a small stuffed bear that had obviously become a favorite dog toy. Raphaela took several additional sips of her tea before setting the cup down and placing the picture and toy in her lap.

The room grew very quiet again, and for a second time, Lyric felt like a low level of electricity was buzzing over her skin. Raphaela shuddered. "They're in a terrible place—filthy, worse than where they were before. There are many more dogs here—all of them dachshunds." Her breath caught in her throat. "Some are very sick, dying. New dogs keep coming. The food lays in urine and feces, the water is almost undrinkable."

Lyric's hand tightened into a fist as tears washed down Anna and John's faces. "What about Emily?" John's voice was a harsh plea.

"There are so many dogs there. In the picture they're sending me, I see more than I can count. Let me ask them to look around."

John leaned forward. Anna put her hand on his arm. He reached over and covered it with his.

"Yes, I see a dog who looks like Emily," Raphaela's voice sounded worried. "She's coughing, like some of the others, and she doesn't want to eat anymore. I've asked Heidi and Gretchen to try and watch over her, to let Emily know that you're searching for her." Her hands tightened for a moment on the stuffed bear.

Lyric leaned forward, changing the direction of the conversation. "Can you tell where they are?"

"I'm looking around now. There's a fence around the yard. The area is quiet, maybe remote. Sometimes a car goes by, but not very often."

"What about the people?"

"I get the impression that the woman has dark hair. It's long, past her shoulders. Her voice is pleasing at first. There is something strange about the man. None of the dogs like his smell. It's different—there's something funny about his skin." Raphaela took a deep breath. "I can't give you more than that." She opened her eyes and handed the photo and stuffed bear back to Anna. When John would have handed her something of Emily's, Raphaela shook her head. "I need to rest now. I can't reach them again today."

Chapter Eleven

"Where the fuck are you?" Kieran asked, once again finding himself standing in front of the snake's habitat. He'd expected his grandmother to bring Lyric back to his house after the... He couldn't even bring himself to think about that bullshit...

What was important was that Lyric should be here, where her car was still waiting out front and where he was waiting inside with a boner that felt like it was going to explode.

Lyric bit her lip and looked around at the mess—no, disaster area—that was Tyler's obviously shared bachelor apartment. What the hell, the worst that could happen by admitting she was here was that Kieran would get it in his mind that she needed to be punished—again. Her nipples went tight at the thought.

Still, no use in making him too crazy. She tempered her answer. "Erin and Cady and I are at Tyler's place."

Kieran's cock jerked in response. He gritted his teeth. "What are you doing there?"

"They got a good lead while I was in Sausalito." The hair stood up along Lyric's neck just remembering Raphaela's description of Leila and Tony. Shit, how could she possibly have known about the woman? Lyric hadn't even known a woman was involved. She'd only found out when she checked her messages and found Erin's excited call. "We're on our way to a breeder's house. She's had contact with the people stealing the dogs. Tyler's going to do a sketch."

"I'll meet you there."

Lyric grimaced. Damn, this was what she was hoping to avoid. If Kieran got involved, then he'd probably insist on being part of the stakeout. And if he saw the Corvette first and followed Leila and Tony back to the dogs, he'd call in the cops, which wasn't a bad idea after the dogs were recovered, but before...the dogs would all get hauled to the shelter and put on a police hold until things were sorted out. Because of the microchips identifying Heidi and Gretchen, Anna would be able to get her dogs back. Maybe with a photo proof of the tear in Emily's ear, John would be able to claim her. But the Jacobsons who had no legal ownership of Angel...and some of the other people that Erin and Cady had told Lyric about...well, tough shit. They'd have to wait, and Lyric didn't like the thought of that.

And for what? Leila and Tony would end up with a slap on the wrists whether the dogs were confiscated or not. The DA wasn't big on animal cases—no glory in them—he was a drug warrior.

Lyric thought there was zero chance that Kieran would agree, but she tried anyway. "Why don't I come to your place afterward and fill you in. No use chewing up your time, too."

Kieran knew he ought to be pissed off, but a laugh escaped. Damn, she was a tricky one. "Nice try, baby. You keep forgetting who's in charge here...and yeah, afterward we'll both come back to my place, and I'll remind you. Give me the address."

Lyric gave him the address and hung up amid snickers. Tyler was the first to speak. "Looks like he has your number, doll. If it's any consolation, I did a little asking around about him. He's got a good rep in the department." His smile widened. "There's also a betting pool running that says he's going to bite the big one and end up related to Bulldog Montgomery."

Lyric's heart lurched and expanded, filling her with a wash of emotions that were as unfamiliar as they were unsettling. She did her best not to let it show. Arching a brow, she said, "I hope you made a smart bet."

Tyler grinned. "I'm counting on the cash. I'll have to rent a tux for the occasion, and knowing the Montgomery family, the reception will look more like a casino in full swing."

Cady laughed and reached over to pull Tyler's hair. "The day Lyric marries a cop is the day you better start worrying that a wedding is in your future."

Erin hid a small smile. Her money was with Tyler's.

"Ready?" Lyric asked, deciding they'd had enough fun with her love life. She wasn't ready to delve too deeply into the thing with Kieran, into the little rush she'd experienced when Tyler mentioned the bet.

"You can ride with us, Tyler, I'll drop you off afterward," Cady said as she turned toward the door, stepping over a pile of dirty clothes in the process. "How can you stand this? Your bedroom was always more organized than any of ours when we were kids."

Tyler kicked the pile of clothes to the side. "Sad truth, Cady, they don't pay police artists a hell of a lot. Besides that, I hate to piss away money renting a place all by myself."

"I still can't believe you're a cop!" Cady tweaked his long blond hair again. "I thought you had to go to the academy to be one. And I thought only vice cops got to wear their hair like this."

Tyler grinned. "Well, I'm not actually a cop. I'm a civilian employee of the police department. Hard for them to insist I cut my hair when they can't ask their women employees to do the same."

Lyric stopped and turned around. Her eyes met Cady's and she knew that they were both thinking the same thing. "Bulldog just bought the house on the other side of Erin's. He hasn't been in a hurry to rent it out." She grimaced. "Actually, he's been trying to get Shane, Braden or Cole to switch houses so we'd have a little more *protection*."

Erin slipped her arm through Tyler's. "Living in one of Bulldog's rentals free of charge is a perk if you work for Crime Tells. I can sketch, but I'm nowhere near as fast or as good as you. And you know that Bulldog is great about us all doing outside work. Even the guys sometimes do other stuff. If you consulted for Crime Tells, I bet you could live in the house. Besides, you're like family already and Bulldog knows you've got other talents besides drawing. It's a winning hand for him—he'll feel like he's pulled out a Royal Flush on the first deal!"

Love washed through Tyler. Damn, the best day of his life was the day they'd settled him into a group home where going to school had led to his making friends with the Montgomery and Maguire kids. "Tell you what, why don't I go see Bulldog and talk to him about it?"

Tyler laughed silently when all three sisters gave him identical frowns and Lyric said, "Does your poker game still suck?"

"Not as royally as it used to."

Cady nibbled on her bottom lip. "Bulldog always says you can tell a lot about a person by the way they play their cards. He plays a hand with everybody he interviews, even potential clients."

"What about Liar's Dice?" Erin asked. "You used to be killer at that."

Tyler grinned. "That's how I make my beer money."

The three sisters smiled and relaxed. "You're in, then," Erin said. "Just be sure to challenge Bulldog to Liar's Dice before he challenges you to poker."

* * * * *

Kieran had been ready to rip Tyler apart when Lyric called from the other man's apartment. But now, seeing Tyler with all three Montgomerys, the jealousy eased and amusement surfaced.

Wily old lady. His grandmother had managed to work it into one of their telephone conversations that Tyler had grown up with Lyric and was almost like a brother. Not that the kiss and hug Kieran had witnessed was brotherly enough to suit him, but seeing the easy affection between Tyler and Cady and Erin, the knot in his gut loosened.

And when Lyric's eyes met his and he read the heated need in them, a need that matched his own, the last of his jealousy faded. She was his woman. She might be a tricky one, but she belonged to him in a way she'd never belonged to another man—in a way that she *would never* belong to another man. They both knew that, though he didn't expect the little hellion to actually admit it—yet. Kieran's heart rate kicked up as he anticipated just how he'd reinforce his claim of ownership when they were alone, but before that, this was an important break, and now that he was thinking rationally, he could admit that having Tyler do some sketches was a good move.

* * * * *

Leila and Tony had come in the red Corvette and acted out the same routine for Barbara and Sam Reed that they'd performed for Mary Jo Rogers. "I can't believe how convincing they were," Barbara said. "After they left, both Sam and I were hoping they'd call back! Leila made us want one of our puppies to go home with her!"

Sam shook his head. "They were convincing all right. Asked the right questions. Made the right moves." He looked at Erin. "After you called, we contacted Mary Jo. Of course we'd heard about her dogs being stolen. It was unnerving hearing her describe Tony and Leila's visit. It was identical, like they were acting out a script. Do you think you'll be able to recover her dogs?"

"We're getting closer," Lyric said. "Finding you was a major break." She smiled at both the Reeds. "That's why there are so many of us here. Besides getting a composite drawing of Leila and Tony, we'll be staking out your place. If they're going to hit, it's probably going to be within the next couple of days."

"We appreciate your efforts," Sam said. "Do you think we should farm out the dogs?"

"If they were my dogs, I would, just to be on the safe side," Lyric answered—not that she thought Leila or Tony would get by her sisters or Kieran, but why risk it?

Barbara shuddered and reached for her husband's hand. "Thank goodness we're down to three puppies and the adult dogs."

"How many adults?" Lyric asked

Barbara directed a nervous look at both Kieran and Tyler. "More than we should have."

Tyler laughed easily and gave Barbara a smile that was designed to set her mind at ease. "Kieran and I don't have any contact with animal control. And today we're here in a very unofficial capacity as a favor to Lyric."

Barbara relaxed. "We've got seven adults here."

Lyric said, "Why don't we go ahead and split up? Kieran and Cady want to check things outside and get a feel for how Leila and Tony would approach the house. The rest of us can go inside. Tyler needs to get started on his drawing and I've got a few more questions to ask."

Barbara hesitated at the front door. "I hate to ask this, but do you mind leaving your shoes here? It's just a precaution against tracking in viruses."

The Reeds' house was small, but comfortable. Barbara led the way to the family room where an exercise pen was set up. Three adorable black and tan puppies immediately rushed over and jumped against the wire, each vying for attention.

"They're precious!" Erin said. "Can I pick them up?"

"Let me spray your hands first." Barbara grabbed a spray bottle from the mantel and misted a pink substance onto Erin's hands and arms. Erin immediately plucked out a puppy and snuggled it against her.

"Want to take a stab at describing Leila and Tony?" Tyler asked Sam.

"Sure. We can do it in here or at the kitchen table."

"Here's fine." Tyler moved over to the sofa and placed his laptop on the coffee table. "Do you have a wireless connection?"

Sam laughed. "Can't live without it!"

"Great."

"Where are the adult dogs?" Lyric asked Barbara.

"In the kitchen. Would you like to see them?"

"Sure." Lyric grinned at the love-fest taking place between Erin and the puppy. They'd be lucky if they got out of there without taking one home with them. "You staying in here?" she asked.

Erin laughed. "That obvious, huh? I forgot how much I missed the unconditional love that comes with these guys! Yeah, I'll stay. I want to watch Tyler do his thing anyway."

Barbara led Lyric down a hallway and into a small kitchen where seven dachshunds immediately surrounded them. "This is Gertie, the mother of the pups," Barbara said with obvious pride as she scooped up a wriggling black dog. "When I was showing her, the judges all just loved her! I got her championship in no time at all."

"She's beautiful." The pup Erin had been holding looked quite a bit like the mother, very gentle and soft in the face.

"And that's Hannah, she's Gertie's full sister." Barbara put Gertie down and pointed to one of the other dogs. "Hannah has a Utility Dog title in Obedience—not an easy accomplishment for a dachshund."

"Not an easy task for a lot of breeds. I was lucky enough to have a poodle when I was growing up. She took to obedience and I showed her all the way through Utility."

Barbara reached down and picked up another dog. "This is Kelly, she's a half sister who just finished her championship. Those two are Juliet and Jac, they aren't related to the puppies. And the two reds are Reno and Nevada."

Lyric shook her head. "You must have zero free time."

Barbara laughed. "None. But it's a labor of love and something Sam and I both enjoy. Before we got into showing dogs, he played golf on the weekends and I shopped. Now we're home together or we're off showing. We have a fully outfitted camper that's like a second home."

"Erin said that you both work during the day. Do you come home for lunch?"

"Rarely. Between the distance and the traffic, by the time either of us gets here, it's time to turn right around and race back. After we spoke to your sister, we both called in and took today off."

"Is this how the dogs are situated when you're gone?"

"Almost. Our garage has been converted to a den/puppy area. Sam built a huge playpen for the puppies and that's where they generally stay when we're not here. The adult dogs are in the kitchen." Barbara pointed to the back door. "We've got a doggie door to the backyard, so they come and go all day. It's a miracle that Erin called us. There's been a raccoon in the neighborhood during the last week. It went through a doggie door and seriously injured a young bulldog puppy. I heard about it when I took Reno in to the vet. So for the last week I've been locking the doggie door, but another neighbor told me just yesterday that they'd been able to trap and relocate the raccoon. Today would have been the first day the dogs could come and go again."

"So when Leila and Tony were here, the door was blocked off?"

"Yes."

"What about your neighbors? Are any of them around during the day?"

"No. They all work."

"Let's see the backyard."

Barbara halted in the process of opening the kitchen door. "Leila asked me those same questions. Not exactly, but close. She even wanted to see how we'd installed the doggie-door, and how we'd blocked it. I should have been suspicious, but she started crying at the thought of losing another dog, especially to a raccoon." A chagrined expression settled on Barbara's face. "I gave her a hug and tried to comfort her, and all the time, she was looking for ways to break in and steal my dogs!"

Barbara's backyard was small, but large enough for the dachshunds. Lyric looked over the fence on either side. The neighbor's yards were also enclosed, and one contained a Doberman. The back fence was a different story. Behind Barbara's house was a bike path leading to a playground. If the timing was right, it would be easy to hop the fence, break in and grab the dogs with very little chance of being seen.

When they returned to the house, Tyler was finished with the sketches. "That's them!" Barbara said as soon as she saw them on the computer screen.

"Did you e-mail them to me?" Lyric asked.

"First thing, then to everyone else, including the Crime Tells address." He winked. "Might as well get used to sending stuff there."

Lyric studied the images. If the picture did Leila justice, then she was certainly model-beautiful. Tony, on the other hand, was one creepy-looking dude.

* * * * *

"What do you think?" Lyric asked as soon as she finished e-mailing Tyler's sketches to Celine.

Kieran backed his car out of the Reeds' driveway and reached over, taking Lyric's hand and placing it on his thigh, just inches away from the bulge in his pants. "I think it's a good thing that we're heading back to my place now."

Lyric edged closer, her hand moving to tease his jeans-covered erection. "That's not what I'm talking about."

He held her hand in place with his. "What I think is that it's a major breakthrough. I'll put in a call to Dasan and Cash later. Between the three of us, we can cover the area pretty well."

"Between the six of us," Lyric corrected.

Kieran grinned. "Now that's where you're wrong, baby. I already laid it out for Cady and she's probably explaining it to Erin right now. You get caught over there, you're going to get hauled down to the police station."

Lyric laughed. "On what grounds?"

"Loitering. Suspicious activity." He squeezed her hand. "Don't worry, baby, you won't do any jail time, but it'll be a pain in your ass sitting around all day while paperwork goes missing."

"That's bullshit!"

"Yeah, it is. But short of handcuffing you to the bed and keeping you there, it's the only way I can think of to keep your beautiful little ass out of trouble." He grinned. "See, baby, I've already got you figured out. I know what would happen if you or your sisters got a fix on that Corvette, and I'm not going to let you get into trouble that way. But this was a good lead, and as soon as we get home, I'll give you a reward for sharing it with me."

"As soon as we get to your house, I'm getting in my car and leaving."

"I don't think so, baby. Remember what I promised this morning?" *Behave yourself today and I'll bring you off with my mouth when we get home.*

Lyric's body pulsed with anticipation. "That was then, this is now, and I'm really pissed at you."

"Your mind may be pissed, but your cunt is all slicked up and your clit is standing at attention just waiting for me." His voice was low and husky. "You want to place a bet, Lyric, on what I'd find if I pulled over and slipped my hand into your panties right now?"

She turned away from him, though he didn't free her hand even when they parked in his driveway. Instead he used it to pull her from the car and into his house. Lyric struggled — not enough that someone would see and call the cops, as if that would do any good — but enough so he knew she wasn't going to just roll over, enough so that both of their hearts were racing by the time the front door closed and he had her pinned against the wall.

"Truth or dare, baby," he said, using one hand to hold her wrists above her head while the other unzipped her jeans and pushed them mid-thigh along with her panties.

Lyric clamped her legs together, fighting him and trying to ease the arousal at the same time. But instead of zeroing in on her engorged clit and labia, on her need-slick channel, his free hand moved to open her shirt and bra.

Her breasts spilled out, the dark nipples still swollen from where he suckled her earlier. Kieran groaned and buried his face against her hot skin. He could barely control himself around her.

When she whimpered and rubbed her breasts against his face, fire shot through his cock. It jerked against the constraint of his jeans.

He licked over an areola and she arched in silent demand for him to suck her. "You still want to leave right now?" He took the nipple between his lips, striking it with the tip of his tongue.

Lyric fought to get closer to him. "No."

"Then tell me what you want."

"You know what I want."

He caught her nipple between his teeth and bit down, just sharply enough to send a blast of fire through her clit. Lyric whimpered and pleaded. "Suck me."

Kieran groaned and fought the urge to ravage her breasts. "Suck what?"

She strained against him, fighting him even as she craved his thorough domination, but the words were forced from her by the need pulsing through her body. "My nipples, my clit. Please, Kieran."

He pulled her to floor and covered her body, this time trapping Lyric's hands at her sides with his. His mouth zeroed in on her breasts and he bit and sucked her nipples, his cock leaking and growing slick in his pants as she thrashed and pleaded and writhed underneath him.

The smell of her arousal filled his nostrils, the need to cover her smooth, bare mound with his mouth a compulsion that Kieran couldn't resist. Groaning he pulled away from her flushed nipples, licking and kissing his way down to her slit, knowing he'd be lost the minute he arrived.

Lyric arched and squirmed, trying to open her legs so that he could bury his face in her cunt, but the waistband of her jeans remained at half-thigh, binding her, preventing her from opening herself to him.

"You'll like this, baby," Kieran said, slipping his tongue in and out between the small space between her thighs, laving her clit with each stroke as he lapped over the swollen folds of her pussy.

Lyric cried out, wanting a deeper penetration. "Oh god, Kieran, please! Don't tease me! Let me come!"

He groaned and pressed his face more tightly to her aroused flesh. His cock felt ready to explode.

"Then come, baby," he ordered, sucking her clit into his mouth, feeding on it as she thrashed and begged and finally screamed when orgasm slammed into her.

Kieran greedily licked up every drop of her sweet release then freed her hands so that he could yank her jeans and panties all the way off. Her channel was still pulsing with orgasm when he freed his cock and shoved it into her with one hard thrust.

"We're not done yet," he said, covering her mouth with his, demanding with a low growl that she accept his tongue, that she suck it in and out just as desperately as her tight channel was doing to his penis. When she complied, white fire raced down his spine, tightening his balls and making him pump harder, faster, slamming against her clit with each stroke until she cried out and the muscles of her cunt gripped him so fiercely that he bucked and spewed and filled her with his seed.

Chapter Twelve

Lyric was seriously considering the merits of pouring a glass of wine and staying in Kieran's hot tub for the rest of the night. She should be pissed that he was off meeting Dasan and Cash so that they could set up a surveillance schedule, but she was just too satisfied. God, she'd known he was trouble as soon as she'd seen him in Anna's doorway.

She grinned. It was a good thing that she liked trouble. And if the completely satisfied look on Kieran's face after he'd fucked her in the hallway was any indication—trouble liked her right back.

Lyric closed her eyes and leaned against the side of the tub, her hands absently smoothing over her flesh. He hadn't been gone that long and already she was starting to need him again. She shivered. She'd experienced lust before, but nothing like this. This was thrilling and scary— a dangerous addiction that she wasn't sure she could fight even if she wanted to.

She should be figuring out a way to cover the Reeds' neighborhood without Kieran making good on his threat to have her hauled to the police station. Instead she was thinking up things they could do to each other in the hot tub.

Lyric enjoyed the fantasies until her cell phone rang. As soon as she saw Celine VanDenbergh's number, adrenaline replaced sexual lassitude.

"Did you get a hit on the drawings I e-mailed?" Lyric asked.

"Not yet, I haven't had a chance to pass them on to anyone. Look, I've only got a few minutes before I head out to cover a zoning committee meeting. My sources at the Animal Freedom Front want to meet you."

A ghost of sensation swirled along Lyric's spine—the kind Grandma Maguire always attributed to someone walking on your grave. "Why?"

"They're thinking about an 'action' if they can get a location for the sale."

"You mean a raid where they go in and take the animals?"

"Liberate them," Celine corrected.

"Why do they want to talk to me?"

"I can't speak for them. But maybe it's because most of the information has come from you so far. Since the Gene Masters action, they've had to be more careful. They're somewhat paranoid about being set up, and you're connected to a lot of people in the crime-solving business."

"When and where?"

"Now. Are you still at your boyfriend's house?"

The ghost of sensation swirling along Lyric's spine grew claws. "Yes."

"There should be a black Cadillac one street over. When you find it, get into the backseat. Don't try and look at the driver. Don't take anything with you other than your keys. Leave your watch at home. And trust me on this, the car is wired for bugs and tracking devices, so make sure you're not fitted with anything. The cops tagged me once, slipped something in my camera case, and it took me almost six months to convince the AFF that I wasn't a plant. If you really want to find those dogs, make sure you're clean. Like I said, they're pretty paranoid right now."

Lyric eased from the hot tub, her gallows humor surfacing. "I'll be clean."

"Talk to you soon. Maybe by then I'll have something on Leila and Tony."

Lyric dried off and pulled on her clothes.

The Caddy was parked where Celine said it'd be, though it left the curb and swung around so the taillights pointed in Lyric's direction. The side view mirrors were folded in, next to the body of the car. Even if she'd been inclined, they wouldn't have provided a view of the driver. A thick barrier of black glass separated the backseat from the front seat. The backseat windows were rolled down, and as soon as she got in and closed the door, the windows slid upward and Lyric understood why they'd been down. The glass contained in them was as dark as the glass separating her from the driver. Except for the ceiling light, it was like being in a tomb with no door handle, no way of opening the window—no way out. When panic threatened to overwhelm Lyric, she pushed it away, concentrating on the car's interior instead.

The seat was black fabric, not leather. At the other end of it were brochures and magazines. She picked them up, sorting through them and finding what she'd expected, AFF publications.

The carpet was also black, but one patch of black on the floor looked different. Lyric reached over and touched the odd spot. Not carpet at all, but a solid black hood. She picked it up and examined it. There was only one opening, where a mouth would be.

Panic surged through her again at the thought of being forced to wear it. This time she forced her head down to her knees and took deep breaths, focusing on what she was after — the dogs.

When you sup with the devil, be sure to use a long spoon... How many times had Grandma Montgomery said that? Lyric shivered, for the first time in her life understanding it all the way down to her gut.

She forced herself to sit up, to stay in control. In the barely lit tomb of the car, there was no way to tell how fast or slow they were going, whether or not they'd gotten on one of the highways or stayed on city streets. With no watch and no sun, with no sounds other than the ones she generated, there was no way of telling how long they'd been driving or how far they'd gone.

It was an effective method of muting reality and she didn't doubt Celine's assertion that the car was loaded with electronics that would expose listening or tracking devices. For all she knew, there were hidden cameras, too, allowing the driver to monitor the passenger. Clever. She'd give the AFF that.

A distorted voice spoke through a speaker when the car finally slid to a halt, ordering her to put the hood on. Lyric's heart jumped — but not uncontrollably this time. She took a deep breath and slipped it over her head.

The passenger door opened and she felt a hand on her upper arm. For a split second, she tensed, but then she forced her muscles to relax and allowed herself to be guided out of the car and forward. The touch on her arm was light, the fingers slender and ringless. A woman, maybe. Somehow that reassured Lyric.

They were in a parking garage, that much she was fairly sure of. The air had the feel and smell of one and her tennis shoes moved over concrete rather than carpet, each step yielding a subtle squeak. She shivered, hyperaware of every sound, every smell, every touch.

The texture changed from concrete to carpet and the hand guided Lyric to a stop. An elevator. There was no mistaking the swoosh of the doors and the ascent. When it stopped, the hand urged her forward and to the left. It had the smell of an office building, not an industrial one.

They stopped, turning to the left again and Lyric could sense that there were other people present—waiting. The door behind her closed quietly but the click echoed along her spine like a gun's report.

The hand led her to a chair, lifting when Lyric had settled in the deep plush seat. A conference room probably. She could feel eyes boring into her, testing her nerve. She almost grinned—not so different than poker, and she had an edge there. Bulldog had been teaching them how to bluff and hold steady since they could tell the difference between an ace and a joker.

A subtle hint of perfume drifted from somewhere in front of Lyric. White Shoulders. She was surprised it was still on the market. One of her aunts used to wear the stuff.

The silence tried to press down on Lyric. It was all she could do to keep from saying, "Throw your ante in or move away from the table so someone else can play."

Finally a man's voice said, "What do you know about the AFF?"

Lyric shrugged. "As much as I want to know. I watch the news. I read Celine's articles. You're wanted by the FBI—probably some other government agencies, too. But you're hard to catch because you're organized into small independent cells, each with a particular animal rights' focus. I assume this one is focused on animal research and testing."

"You know that we don't believe in exploiting animals, and that includes keeping them as pets?"

Lyric had forgotten that part of their doctrine. "Yeah, that fits."

"Besides working for your grandfather's detective agency, you make your living finding and returning animals to captive situations."

"And you're suggesting they're better off being hit by cars, starving, or being euthanized at animal shelters?" There was no apology in her voice.

"Do you believe that animals are better off because of their association with mankind?"

Lyric shrugged. "In the big picture—factoring in all the throwaway and mistreated animals, plus the ones that end up on dinner tables—no, but don't sign me up for your cause. I'm not going there."

There was a muffled laugh, feminine, followed by the light scratching sound of someone writing. "You've got a reputation for being willing to break the law when it comes to your clients," the male voice said.

"I do what I have to do."

"Just as we do. You know that we were responsible for the liberation of the Gene Masters animals?"

"Hard to miss that fact. It made a big splash on the news, plus Celine did an in-depth article."

There were several muted snickers. Two of them came from directly in front of Lyric, several more from behind and to the side.

"It was a real coup for us," the man said.

No shit. But Lyric was curious. "What did you do with the animals you…liberated?"

"Some were in such terrible shape that we euthanized them. The remainder now live in a sanctuary—with minimal human contact."

Lyric frowned, her thoughts leaping to a logical conclusion and not liking what she saw—a losing hand. "So if you raid the auction and the dachshunds are there, they'll end up with the other animals, at some sanctuary?"

More scribbling on paper. "It depends." Then silence.

Like an actress saying her lines, Lyric asked, "It depends on what?"

"On whether or not you participate in the action."

Oh shit—big trouble. Huge fucking trouble. "What do you mean…exactly?"

"A related action will be taking place shortly. When it does, we'll get a call from our associates. Hopefully in the course of their action, they'll be able to discover the location of the upcoming sale. We've decided to liberate the animals, regardless of whether or not you go with us. If you join the action, then all of the dachshunds will be turned over to you. If you choose not to go, then the animals will gain permanent sanctuary with us."

"What would I have to do?"

More scribbling. "Observe, help load animals into our trucks if you want. Celine will be there recording the event. You could stay close to her if you wanted."

The silence descended again, pressing down on Lyric, harder to ignore now. It was time to fold and walk away or call their bet and see the game played out. In her mind there was only one choice. "I'll go."

Chapter Thirteen

The Caddy dropped Lyric off in Kieran's neighborhood. It was a different street, opposite side and to a right angle from the one he lived on, but Lyric found her way back to his house. Relief washed through her when she saw that his car was still gone. She was even more relieved when she settled in front of his TV and caught the news—the AFF action in LA was a broad daylight raid, liberation, and subsequent torching of a company called Bio-Specimens.

Shit. Had she led them to it when she asked Celine to trace the license plate of Tony's white truck? Or had they already known the location?

Lyric picked up the phone and dialed Celine, willing to play a game of pretend if it got her answers. "You saw the news?" she asked as soon as the reporter answered.

Celine laughed. "Yes, scooped by other reporters, but I guess I can't cover every story like that one. Today I've been buried under stories about ambitious politicians and suspicious zoning changes."

Oh yeah. Like I'm going to believe that one. "Anything on the pictures of Tony and Leila?"

"Half and half. Tony's new on the scene. My contacts don't know anything about him. But Leila has been around a long time."

"What do they have on her?"

"She's bad news. Here's what I have. Leila Price. Grew up in the Midwest, small town. The closest big city is Omaha. When she was eighteen her parents died in a suspicious house fire. The police could never prove anything though they did take her in for questioning. As soon as she could, she cleaned out her parents' bank accounts and headed to LA. Probably thought she would be a natural for Hollywood."

Lyric grimaced. "Her and a million girls just like her."

"True, I'm glad it's not my beat. No way of knowing for sure, but my guess is that Leila was running out of her parents' money when she hooked up with a sugar daddy named…hmmm…I can't get my hands on that. But he was four times her age and died about six months after hooking up with her. It was ruled a heart attack, but he had a clean bill of health. Adult children tried to get the police to look into it, but they declined and Leila walked away with enough money to keep her in style for a couple more years."

"When that ran out, she settled for a guy named Leroy Bruttel. Twice her age and big-time scum. He used to drive around in a chauffeured limo and pull out a roll of bills to impress anybody who was looking. It was before I landed this job, but my contacts at the AFF say that they celebrated when Bruttel was killed. From what they tell me, he'd done it all — puppy-milling, greyhound racing, pit bull fighting, setting up 'big-game' hunts with 'retired' circus and zoo animals — and of course, bunching."

"What happened to him?"

"Drive-by shooting. No witnesses, no suspects, no arrests."

Lyric wasn't going to touch that one. "And Leila?"

"Started out as his bed buddy, then must have seen how easy the money came in. By the time Leroy died, Leila was a full partner."

"So she's based in LA?" Lyric's mind flipped back to the speed-amped man at Bio-Specimens. He'd called his boss *her*—Lyric would bet money that his boss was Leila Price.

"Was, might still be. She's kept a low profile for the last year or so. I'm not sure exactly what happened, but there's another guy down in LA who's in the same line of work. The two of them had some kind of run-in and since people who aggravate Julio tend to end up somewhere in the Pacific Ocean, Leila's stayed out of sight."

"Dead end for now."

"Seems that way."

Lyric let silence open up on the line, giving Celine a chance to volunteer that Leila Price was the force behind Bio-Specimens—although not really expecting her to—but when the reporter didn't say anything else, Lyric ended the call.

* * * * *

Kieran felt edgy as hell by the time he parked in front of his house. If Lyric's source was right and the sale was tomorrow and Saturday, then Leila and Tony would hit tomorrow or not at all since the Reeds would be home on the weekends.

He didn't like having everything resting on one lead, on one stakeout. Fuck, for all they knew, Tony and Leila already had enough dogs, maybe that's why they hadn't hit the Reeds' place yet. Or maybe they'd cut a side deal and were shipping the dogs separately. Shit, maybe it was already too late.

It was like looking for a fucking needle in a haystack and Kieran was allergic to that kind of a case. Christ, he felt like he was about to go through his skin.

He pushed into the house, not sure what he needed until he saw Lyric. And then the blood raced to his cock as lust swirled like a tornado inside of him. She met his gaze with a knowing one of her own.

"Looks like you need to blow off some steam," she said, stripping out of her shirt without being told.

The breath left Kieran's body in a pant at the sight of her tight dark nipples. She covered them with her fingers, tweaking and tugging, making his penis pulse and twitch to her rhythm.

"You're playing with fire, baby."

The little hellion smiled as she pulled her hands away from her breasts and unzipped her jeans, letting them join her shirt on the floor. She moved tanned fingers over her smooth mound, running them over her clit and sliding them between her legs. "I can handle you, Kieran."

Son of a bitch. He could see her wet arousal. Smell it.

"Baby, unless you want to be fucked where you stand, you'd better start running."

She laughed and ran, bolting down the hallway and into the TV room. Kieran chased, adrenaline surging through him, the only thought in his mind to catch her and mount her.

He trapped her behind the couch and forced her to lean over its back and spread her legs. Her cunt glistened, its lips plump and open, an invitation that had him ripping his pants down and shoving his cock into her with a desperate frenzy.

One hand moved to cup her mound, to rub against her clit in time to his pounding thrusts. *Mine! Mine! Mine!* echoed through every cell as he plunged in and out of her wet sheath, victorious in his claiming, in the feel of her spasming against him, screaming his name as she came, as she demanded with her body that he give her everything.

White fire ripped through his balls and cock, exploding out in a release that left him humping through their combined juices even after he'd spent his seed. Christ, he would never get enough of her.

It had to be God's little joke, Kieran thought as he studied Lyric's sleeping form. She looked like an angel when she slept, a dark one, but an angel all the same.

He'd thought his life was full until she came along. He loved his job, his family, hell, not that he'd admit it out loud, but he even loved his partner. He stayed busy, ended most days feeling satisfied. It was a good life.

He hadn't known what he was missing.

A fist squeezed his heart and he leaned over to brush a kiss against her temple. Fuck. He was in unfamiliar territory here.

One way or another, this case was coming to an end. He'd have to get back to work, she'd move on to helping other clients.

He hated the thought of her not being here when he got home in the evenings. It wasn't just the sex, though that was reason enough to want her in his house.

Kieran closed his eyes for a second, sensations bombarding him as he remembered the way she'd gone down on him in the shower after they'd made love for a second time in the TV room. Damn. The little hellion was perfect for him. They were perfect for each other. He just had to find a way to get her to stay that didn't involve cuffing her to the bed—his cock twitched and he grinned—not that he was entirely opposed to that idea.

Her nipple caught his attention and he moved, ready to take it in his mouth, to tease her into waking up so that he could have her again, but before he could follow-through, his cell phone vibrated against the wood of the nightstand. He eased away from Lyric, careful not to wake her as he reached for the phone and saw the caller ID. Cash.

"Yeah," Kieran whispered, already slipping from the bed.

"We're on. The 'Vette just drove by Dasan."

Kieran escaped the bedroom, grateful he'd left his clothes where they landed in the TV room last night. She was tricky enough to follow him if she woke up before he was gone.

"How many in the car?"

"One. The woman."

That surprised Kieran. "Dasan get a plate number?"

"Yeah, Los Angeles address. Bio-Specimens, which isn't going to do us a hell of a lot of good right now."

Something about the name nudged at the edge of Kieran's mind, but Cash chased it away by saying. "She's pulled over near the playground. You on your way?"

"Just getting out of the house."

Cash laughed. "Sneaking out of your own place?"

"Yeah, Lyric's asleep."

"You have it bad, partner."

Kieran grimaced but didn't say anything. Cash laughed again. "Dasan just radioed that Leila's out of her car. Stick with the plan, let her break in, then follow her?"

"Yeah. Dasan's outfitted with a camera?"

"Never leaves home without one."

Kieran rolled his eyes. Cash rarely missed a chance to live up to his reputation as a smart ass.

"What's your ETA?" Cash asked.

"I'll hit the freeway exit in about ten minutes."

"Good. Hope we're right and she's going to bolt to the south."

"Unless she's picking up another batch of dogs, I think it's a good bet."

"Okay, she's over the fence. I'm getting in position to start the tail."

Adrenaline was rushing through Kieran, making the wait for fresh information almost unbearable. Finally Cash said, "She's a smart one. Dasan says she figured out that there aren't any dogs in the house as soon as she started trying to open the dog door. Probably didn't hear any barking. She stood up and knocked to make sure. Now she's heading back to her car and checking the area. She's wondering if someone's on to her. Good thing we're going to run a pattern."

"Yeah, good thing."

"All right, she's in her car, I'll call you back once we've got a fix on which way she's going."

* * * * *

Lyric came awake to the sound of her cell phone ringing in the hallway. She scrambled to where she'd left her jeans pooled on the floor and grabbed the phone.

Celine. "I'm just turning on to your boyfriend's street. Leave everything but your keys." The phone went dead and there was just enough time for Lyric to get her clothes on before a white car pulled up in front of the house.

Lyric went outside, instantly aware that Kieran's car was gone. Her skin was humming, but she didn't know whether it was Celine's presence or the possibility that Leila and Tony had been spotted at the Reeds' house.

No choice now but to play the cards the way they landed. She moved down the walkway and got into Celine's BMW.

The reporter wasn't what Lyric expected. Between the name and the voice, she'd imagined long hair and feminine features. Instead, Celine was almost mannish—with a narrow, hawkish-face and brown-gray hair cut in a severe style. But as soon as Lyric slipped into the car, the hint of White Shoulders hit her. Now *that* she had expected.

"Nervous?" Celine asked, giving Lyric a small, one-side-of-her-mouth smile.

Lyric shrugged. "I haven't hit the adrenaline rush stage."

"You will. This is the fourth AFF action I've photographed, believe me, you'll feel the rush."

"I assume that you caught the fact that the cell in LA torched Bio-Specimens when they were done."

Celine shrugged. "It was a nice piece of work. But don't worry, there won't be any fires. This sale is taking place out-of-doors. The cell members wouldn't start something that could get out of control and hurt the wildlife."

The reporter eased the BMW onto Highway 101 and traveled south. "We'll stop at a friend of mine's house and wait for the cell members to pick us up."

"How long?"

She shrugged. "I don't know. They don't share any more information than they have to."

A little over an hour and a half later Celine exited the highway, crisscrossing back and forth until she came to a wrought iron gate. She plucked a remote-control box off of her window visor. A quick punch of a button and the gate swung open. They pulled through and continued past seven ranch-style houses on huge lots.

"Nice," Lyric said.

"My friend thinks so." Celine pulled into a driveway and hit another button, this one opened the garage door. "We'll wait here until it's time to go. The others are assembling somewhere else."

The house had high ceilings and very few walls. "You want something to drink?" Celine asked. "We've probably got several hours of waiting ahead of us. I'm going to have a glass of orange juice, but there are some sodas here, too."

"Sure. I'll have a glass of the juice."

Celine moved around to the bar. "Look, I probably shouldn't tell you this. But the cell members are divided on whether or not to let you have the dachshunds."

Lyric's heartbeat shot through her eardrums. "Then why am I here?"

Celine poured the glasses of orange juice. "As far as I've been able to tell, they operate under democratic principles. I think the faction that's willing to let you take the dogs wants to give you a chance to convince the ones who don't."

"And how am I supposed to do that?"

Celine eyebrows drew together in a good imitation of someone trying to work something out. "I think it depends on what happens when we get to the auction," she said slowly, wanting Lyric to believe it was a spontaneous thought and not a calculated conversation. "If you don't participate other than to help with the animals, then they'll probably vote no. If you do anything—even spray-paint AFF on some of the cars or break a few windshields, then they'll probably vote in your favor."

When you sup with the devil, be sure to use a long spoon. Lyric turned to the window to avoid Celine's hawk-like focus and bird of prey intensity.

A broken windshield, a slash of paint—it wouldn't stop there. Slowly but surely they'd entangle her more fully in their web. Shit, she couldn't even begin to guess why they wanted her—not when there were others more than willing to become enmeshed.

Was it wrong to steal from a thief? To hustle a hustler? To kill a killer? Situational ethics had always been Lyric's trump card. But she couldn't lay it down here.

Anna and John and the others would have to find peace with the knowledge that their dogs were safe. She turned from the window and looked at Celine. "I won't play that hand."

Celine moved over and handed Lyric the glass of juice. "You're a straight shooter. I'll argue your case when they call." She touched her glass to Lyric's. "To a good raid, and to getting your dogs back."

* * * * *

The red Corvette pulled into a driveway, paused, then squealed backward and shot down the street past Kieran. His stomach roiled, his temper was one second from blowing. "What the fuck?" They'd been jockeying positions on and off for over an hour so that she wouldn't see the same car behind her. Shit!

The cellular rang. "What's going on?" Cash said. "She make you? She just flew by me like the cops were on her tail."

Kieran whipped his car into the same drive and paused at the sight that greeted him. *Liberated by the Animal Freedom Front!* was spray-painted across the front of the house in red. Fuck! That's where he'd heard the name Bio-Specimens before. He'd heard it on the news. The Animal Freedom Front had broken in, taken the animals and then torched the place. Shit!

"Kieran. You there? In another minute she's going to whip right past Dasan." Cash's voice sounded tense. "Should we follow?"

"Fuck. Yeah. Tell Dasan to follow. Goddamn. I think we're too late."

"What? Shit Kieran, what's going on? I'm just turning at the Flea Market. How far away are you?"

"Two or three miles. Right-hand side. You'll see my car. I'm going in."

Kieran closed his cellular and got out of the car. He didn't bother trying the front door. The stench coming from the backyard already told him what he wanted to know. He drew his gun and moved around, halting as soon as he'd gone through the side gate.

Fuck. Shades of the same cesspool he'd found at Rickard's place, and not a dog in sight.

A car squealed to a halt in the driveway and a door slammed. Cash.

"Kieran!"

"Around back."

His partner joined him. "Goddamn!"

"Yeah, and them some."

"You see the graffiti on the front of the house?"

"Yeah. It's out here, too."

Cash stalked to the open back door and looked inside. "We've got probable cause. I'm going in." Before he could enter the house the radio on his belt chirped and a long stream of Dasan's curses followed. "She got past me. Jumped through a red light and left me locking up my brakes to keep from hitting a semi. You want me to backtrack?" Cash looked to Kieran.

Kieran shook his head. "Tell him what we've got here. He might as well join us."

Cash relayed the information then went into the house. Kieran followed a minute later. What could be broken, was broken. Any surface that could be spray-painted, was spray-painted.

"The Feds will want a piece of this," Cash said.

Kieran shrugged. "There won't be anything here for them." He forced himself to go through the motions of checking for any clue to where Leila, Tony, or the dogs might be.

Dasan came in just as Kieran and Cash came back out. His face looked every bit as grim as their faces did. "You call it in yet?" he asked.

"Shit," Kieran growled. "We'll be tied up here all fucking day."

Dasan shook his head. "I've got a friend in the department down here. I'll call it in and tell him that we can't stick. He can track us down later if he wants." The bounty hunter looked around. "Not a place you want to leave any DNA or trace that can't be explained away. Feds will be all over this one."

They moved around the side of the house, heading for their cars. "You check the garbage cans?" Dasan asked.

"No time yet," Cash said and they moved over to the cluster of plastic garbage containers.

"Exhibit A, rotten garbage." Kieran stood up an open garbage can that had been lying on its side, adding to the stench.

"Exhibit B," Cash said. "Confetti ala paper-shredder."

Kieran snorted as he lifted the lid on the third. "Aluminum cans. Maybe they'll come back and get these so they can get their deposit back." He slammed the lid down, pissed all over again.

A low canine whimper startled all of them and had them searching through the garbage that had escaped from the downed trashcan.

"Shit, here it is," Cash said.

Kieran's throat tightened at the sight of the small red body. Fuck, he couldn't tell whether it was one of his grandmother's dogs or not.

Cash eased his hands under the dog and stood. "Female." His face was somber when he looked at Dasan. "Any ideas?"

"Get her to my van." He cut a glance at Kieran. "You recognize her?"

Kieran shook his head. "No. I'm not sure I would, not like this."

* * * * *

Lyric woke up in the tomb of the Caddy—disoriented, pissed, queasy.

"Sorry," Celine said. "If it's any consolation. My orange juice was drugged, too, self-administered. With Gene Masters offering a huge reward, the AFF is very cautious."

Lyric straightened away from where she was leaning against the window and studied Celine. The reporter's eyes had the dilated look of someone who'd been knocked out.

Maybe she had, maybe she hadn't. It gave Lyric a new appreciation for the intellect she was dealing with.

Celine handed Lyric a long-sleeved red t-shirt exactly like the one she was wearing, then a black mask—this one with both eye and mouth holes—along with a pair of black gloves. "Put the shirt on now, the gloves and hood can wait until we're ready to get out of the car."

The cellular radio Celine wore on her hip squawked, chasing away the last of the drugs in Lyric's system. A man said, "It's up ahead. Do you see it?"

Another said, "I see it."

"We're close," Celine said. "They'll secure the place first, then we'll go in."

The cellular chirped again. "The guards have been neutralized. Lead Vehicles One and Two proceeding."

Raw fear whipped through Lyric's system. "Neutralized?"

Celine laughed. "Tranqed with a dart gun, though some of the members do carry live weapons."

The radio squawked. "Coming into range. Action to commence momentarily. Get ready."

Celine lifted her hood and slipped it on. Lyric changed her shirt and did the same.

Chapter Fourteen

"Lead Vehicle One and Two are trucks loaded with AFF members. They'll swarm on the sellers and subdue them—with the dart guns mostly. Then they'll blindfold them and use duct tape to secure them," Celine said as she picked up her camera and checked the settings. "As soon as that's done, they'll split into teams. Each team has a specific task—guarding, loading the animals, and chaos." She sent Lyric another hawk-like glance. "Chaos is the trademark of this cell. They'll wreck anything useful and spray-paint messages so the buyers and sellers will understand that animal testing isn't going to go on in a 'business as usual' way."

The cellular radio buzzed with static before a man's voice said, "All secured. Bring the reporter and the witness in."

Celine gave the thumbs-up sign and reached for her gloves. "Here we go."

The scene that greeted Lyric was part military operation, part nightmare. Armed AFF members stood guard over twice as many buyers and sellers, while barks and whimpers filled the air.

Hooded AFF members were already loading animals into trucks. The whir and click of Celine's camera was a constant as Lyric scanned the area, uneasiness filling her when she didn't see Tony or Leila.

Celine paused, nudging Lyric and pointing—the telephoto lens on her camera giving her an advantage. Lyric nodded and headed toward a battered white truck. When she got closer, she saw that the wire crates stacked four-high next to it were full of small dogs. The bottom crate contained dachshunds.

Lyric joined the hooded figure who was reaching for the top crate—the very listlessness of the animals inside the cages warning her that they were close to becoming dissection specimens. Two additional members stopped, taking the second and third cages as the first member returned. Lyric grabbed the crate containing the dachshunds—raw horror washing over her with the realization that one of listless, sick dogs in the cage was a red female with a notch in her ear. Emily.

She turned toward the Caddy, but the black-hooded figure crowded into her space, taking hold of one end of the cage and using Lyric's own refusal to let go to maneuver her to a place where she could see inside the truck where the other crates had been loaded.

IV bags hung from hooks on the walls. As Lyric watched, AFF members opened crates and triaged the animals, separating the dead from the living, placing some of the dogs on tables bolted to the walls, working over them with the precision of veterinarians in a clinic.

Lyric nodded. There was no choice. The hooded figure let her take the cage to the truck. She stayed long enough to see Emily gently placed on the table with an IV in her thin, tiny body.

Without a scanner, there was no way of knowing if Anna's dogs were among the sick…or dead. Emotion tightened into a hard knot in Lyric's throat. There'd only been about fifteen dogs in the cage, way short of the number that should be there.

Lyric joined other black-hooded figures heading to a long string of dogs, each tethered to a chain. Some of the dogs were so thin that they looked like skeletons. Others had gone past the point where they could endure—their eyes were blank, showing not even a flicker of interest when Lyric unchained them, guiding them into crates so they could be safely transported.

She paused at a Doberman that had just about chewed his own leg off—the bone and muscle tissue exposed, covered now with flies instead of skin. Two neighboring Shepherd-mixes had fought until one lay more dead than alive—a gaping wound slashed across his neck—a pool of blood under him. An AFF member with a syringe of euthanasia formula motioned for Lyric to move on.

She joined other members, helping them to remove stacks and stacks of crated animals. By the time the last cage of dogs was loaded into a truck, she was nearly frantic, her stomach sick both at what she'd seen, and not seen. There'd only been a few more dachshunds, mixed in with other dogs, and most likely not collected by Leila.

The cats were the last animals to be loaded. Covered in urine and feces, the dead with the living—they were stuffed into cages so tightly that they could barely move. Only sheer determination kept Lyric from vomiting.

When it was done, she moved back to Celine's side. She was ready to leave, to claim Emily and the dachshunds found here then start looking for Tony and Leila and the rest of the dogs. She was anxious to get the hell out of here and away from the AFF. The rage boiling through her was only just barely under control. It would be easy to pick up a sledgehammer and wreak havoc—to join them and create chaos.

As she and Celine moved toward the Caddy, some primitive form of self-preservation brought Lyric's head around. There was a quick flash of light and movement where the sellers' cars and trucks were parked. Shock froze Lyric's heart for a beat when the cold pale blue of Tony's eyes collided with hers. The gun in his hand fired in the same instant that she pushed Celine.

They both fell in a heap on the ground. There was a shout and several of the armed members took off after Tony. Celine scrambled to her feet. "You've been hit!"

Disbelieving, Lyric looked down at her side. There was a hole in the red t-shirt and as she watched, blood oozed out of the opening.

"Get Gary," Celine said, an order not a request, as she pressed her hand down on the wound to slow the bleeding. A few minutes later an AFF member was kneeling next to Lyric. The numbness in her side had edged into pain sharp enough to make her sweat and cry out when he peeled the bloody shirt up.

"Looks like the bullet grazed a rib as it went through. Needs some stitches. We can take care of it in one of the Op Trucks."

"Good," Celine said.

Lyric almost passed out when Gary lifted her and carried her to a truck filled with armed men and women still wearing hoods and gloves. "Get a tarp on the floor," he said, and without being told, one of the members put a towel on the tarp. Gary eased Lyric down and stripped off the red t-shirt. "Don't worry, this'll be incinerated—

someone's probably already bleaching the place you went down. We don't leave DNA evidence around."

"Thanks," Lyric managed through the waves of pain and nausea.

"Are you allergic to any medications?"

"No."

"Any medical history that I should know about, your own or your family members?"

"No."

The truck lurched forward and began moving. A radio chirped. "Phase two of disengagement has commenced. Exit team has disabled enemy vehicles. Animals now en route to secure location." A small cheer went up.

Gary retrieved a syringe from a black doctor's bag. "I'm going to give you a painkiller now."

A burst of static preceded another progress report. "Drivers to break away and proceed to debriefing point separately. Op Truck One and Civilian Transport continue to designated rendezvous point."

Uneasiness ripped through Lyric as Gary leaned over her with the syringe—the image of a black-masked figure hovering above the Doberman with a lethal dose of euthanasia formula flashed in her mind. She struggled to sit up, but was held down as blood poured from her side. "No!"

Gary paused. "It's just a bit of morphine. It won't knock you out if that's what you're worried about."

Lyric shook her head, not willing to trust him, not willing to lose control. "No."

He hesitated. "Okay. Let me know if you change your mind."

She almost did by the time he'd stitched up her side and ordered the driver to pull over so she could be transferred back to Celine and the Caddy.

"She didn't want to be knocked out," Gary said as they settled Lyric on the seat.

Celine's eyes met and held his. "She needs an antibiotic shot at least. She can't take the chance of going to a doctor. There are too many witnesses who saw her go down."

"No shots," Lyric said, gritting her teeth against the pain. Bulldog would know who she could call—hell, Kieran would probably know who she could see without worrying about the gunshot wound being reported.

When Gary returned with the medical bag, he brought help. "It's for your own good," Celine murmured, her hands pressing against Lyric's forehead, helping to keep her pinned as Gary quickly wrapped a rubber tube around Lyric's arm and stabbed a needle into her vein.

The pain disappeared quickly, along with consciousness.

Chapter Fifteen

Erin's heart just about stopped when she walked into Crime Tells and saw Lyric stretched out on the couch, her shirt pushed up to expose a length of white bandage wrapped around her ribs.

"Lyric!"

Lyric opened her eyes, somehow managing a small smile. "Couldn't call. Didn't want to try and get up and land on my ass instead. I'm glad to see you."

"What happened?"

"You don't want to know."

Erin was more than ready to argue that point when her attention was caught by a small baggie on the floor. She scooped it up. "You've been shot." Hell, when she'd been a cop, she'd seen more than her share of shell casings and spent bullets.

"Shit," Lyric muttered. She didn't remember being transferred from the Caddy to Celine's car, didn't remember anyone mentioning that they'd retrieved the bullet or the casing. She only barely remembered Celine helping her into the office and onto the couch. God only knew what Erin would do. "Give me that."

"Not a chance, baby sister."

Lyric tried to stall the inevitable. "If you give me a lecture, I probably won't remember it. I'm still a little out of it." The truth was that whatever drugs they'd pumped into her system were starting to fade, but Lyric was willing to try and bluff her way through this. She needed to call Celine, to put the pressure on if that's what it would take to get the dogs. She'd taken a bullet for Celine, and she'd use that as her trump card if she could.

Erin stood. "I'm not going to give you a lecture. That would be pointless!" She stalked over to her desk, angry concern radiating from every pore and making Lyric feel guilty.

The guilt turned into near panic when Erin picked up the phone, punched in a number and began speaking almost immediately. "She's at the office, Kieran. She's been shot."

* * * * *

Dasan followed in Kieran's wake, careful not to get between Kieran and his objective. Too bad Cash wasn't here to see this. He'd enjoy it, especially since it was happening to someone else and Lyric wasn't in any danger.

The way Dasan saw it, if someone had bothered to patch her up, get her to Crime Tells, and leave the evidence of what happened with her, then the injury probably wasn't life-threatening. He hadn't bothered trying to tell that to Kieran—hell, he hadn't had time.

They'd taken the dog to Anna's vet, then moved on to Kieran's house—with Cash taking a detour to the police station in order to work a shift. Dasan laughed silently at the memory of Kieran stomping around his house and cursing because Lyric wasn't there, wasn't at his grandmother's house and wasn't with either of her sisters. Each fresh wave of ranting began and ended with Kieran standing in front of the snake's cage.

Fitting. But Dasan didn't share that thought with Kieran either.

Even if they were sitting around a bar drinking, he doubted that Kieran would want to hear why the snake was in his home. What having such a powerful totem choose to touch your life meant. How that touch expanded outward, like a spider's web, weaving fates together.

Nah, Kieran wasn't any more open to that kind of conversation than Cash was. Dasan mentally shrugged. Open or not, it didn't matter.

He followed Kieran into Crime Tells, his heart almost stopping when he saw Lyric's sister wearing an intricately carved representation of the Great Feathered Sky Serpent on a delicate silver chain around her neck. The sign offered by his totem spirit couldn't be any clearer.

Kieran wanted to pound on something, on someone, when he saw the stark white bandage against Lyric's skin. "What happened? Who shot you? Where the hell have you been?"

"You don't want to know."

"The fuck I don't!" He snatched the plastic baggie containing the ballistic evidence out of Erin's hands and waved it in front of Lyric's face. "Start talking, baby, you're in some serious shit here!"

"It'd be better if you didn't know. It'd keep you one step removed, give you plausible deniability and all of that."

Kieran felt like his head was going to explode. When he got her home... The glaring white of her bandage stopped him. Fuck, he had to know how bad this was. His gaze moved to Dasan. The man's van was like an armed services first aid unit. It was probably the only reason they'd been able to save the dog they'd found with the trash. Shit. He kept getting in deeper and deeper, feeling less and less in control. "You have any experience with bullet wounds?"

The bounty hunter's eyebrows rose. "You want me to take a look at her?"

Kieran nodded and knelt down next to Lyric. She laughed. "Getting your friend to clear me before we go a round?"

"Yeah." His voice told her that they *would* go a round and he *would* have answers.

She turned her attention to the man who'd moved closer and now hovered above her. "Are you Cash or Dasan?"

"Dasan." He removed a knife from his pocket and flicked it open. Lyric braced for the cold feel of the blade against her skin. Her side ached, but it was nothing like the pain she'd experienced when she first got shot.

Dasan peeled the bandage back and Lyric's gaze went immediately to the neat stitches holding her flesh together. The skin around the stitches was bruised and raw, but even to her inexperienced eye, everything looked good.

"Nice work," Dasan said. He looked at Kieran. "Somebody knew what they were doing." Turning back to Lyric he asked, "How's the pain?"

"More of a deep ache than anything else."

"I've got something in the van that'll numb the area and speed up the healing process, just don't forget you've got stitches and break them open doing something vigorous." There was just the hint of amusement in his dark eyes as he rose.

Lyric's gaze moved to Kieran and the fierce, unrelenting, you've-gone-too-far-this-time look on his face. Somehow she doubted that he was contemplating a punishment that included vigorous sex. She'd give him a day or two to come around.

"Start talking," he growled.

Her heart lurched. Or not.

Lyric closed her eyes briefly. Shit, unless she was dealing with scum, she'd always been pretty much a straight shooter. She didn't want to start lying now, not to him, not to Erin—though her sister might just as soon *not* know.

As if reading her thoughts, Erin tightened her jaw. "You owe it to us to tell us what happened, Lyric. We're all involved in this case."

Lyric groaned and not from the pain in her side. Erin could guilt an innocent man into confessing.

"I was at the sale. The AFF knew I was looking for the dachshunds and contacted me. They raided the sale. They offered me a chance to get the dogs back if I went as a witness. So I went. There were only about fifteen or twenty dachshunds. Emily was there. I don't know about Anna's dogs, or where the rest of them are."

Kieran exploded. "Goddammit, Lyric! I can't fucking believe you!" Son of a bitch, he wanted to grab her and shake some sense into her. Goddamn! What was he going to do with her? "I cannot fucking believe this!"

Dasan came back in and leaned over Lyric, effectively ending the rant as he slathered something that smelled like the desert over her skin. Almost instantly the pain disappeared. "Try to go without a bandage if you can."

Lyric eased herself into a sitting position just as Dasan snapped the lid shut on the small tin containing the salve and handed it to her. When she saw that the container had once held mints, her curiosity was piqued. "Do you make this stuff?"

Dasan nodded. It was one of the many secrets handed down from shaman father to shaman son.

Kieran gritted his teeth. He didn't give a fuck about Dasan's salve. He wanted answers. "Tell me everything. Now."

For a long minute Lyric's heart stuttered in her chest. She didn't regret what she'd done, couldn't regret it—and yet looking at Kieran's tense, all-cop face, she knew that it might have cost her him.

She told him anyway, not everything—though she suspected that he'd keep digging until he had it all—but enough. With each word his expression grew more closed and her soul filled with sadness. A heavy silence reigned when she'd finished.

Dasan broke it by saying, "So the AFF has all the dachshunds now. If there were only about twenty dogs at the sale, then they must have found Leila and Tony's address when they broke into Bio-Specimens. That's how they beat us to the dogs."

Realization dawned on Lyric. "You tailed the Corvette from the Reeds' house."

Dasan nodded. "Right to Leila's place and if her reaction was anything to go by, she was just as shocked as we were that the AFF had been there. They left their calling card spray-painted across the front of her house."

Erin spoke for the first time, her voice steady though Lyric could see that she was upset. "So now we wait and see if the AFF votes to release the dogs?"

Lyric wanted to get up and hug her sister, to tell her not to worry so much. But she could tell that Erin was close to tears. One hug and Erin would lose it, and that would only make it worse for her sister. Erin would hate to lose control in front of Kieran and Dasan. So Lyric said, "Yeah, we wait," though she intended to call Celine as soon as she was alone. That was the only information that she'd held back—her suspicions about just how deeply the reporter was involved with the AFF.

Lyric pushed up from the sofa, the pain in her side nonexistent, the pain in her heart like shards of jagged ice as the coldness remained in Kieran's expression. "We might as well take a breather for a while," she said. "Can you give me a lift home, Erin?"

Before her sister could answer, Kieran's hand circled Lyric's wrist and tightened in warning. "You're coming with me."

Erin began crying as soon as Kieran guided Lyric through the door, her wrist shackled by his hand like a bad omen. God, she'd been so scared as she'd listened to Lyric talk. She was still scared. What if Lyric ended up in jail over this? What if... Warm arms surrounded Erin and pulled her against a strong, muscled body, offering comfort when she was too weak to resist.

A tender protectiveness filled Dasan as he held Erin in his arms and rubbed his cheek over soft, golden curls until her tears subsided. She let him hold her for a few heartbeats longer, then embarrassment rippled through her and she pulled away, blushing and uncomfortable, her vulnerability a love-tipped arrow that went straight to his heart.

"Sorry," she said, straightening her spine. "Usually I don't fall apart like that, but sometimes...sometimes I get scared for Lyric."

Dasan wanted to pull her back in his arms, to kiss and protect and comfort her. Instead he said, "I don't think you'll have too much to worry about in the future. Kieran's probably laying down the law right now."

Erin hiccupped a laugh. "You don't know much about my sister, do you? Sometimes that only makes it seem like a more exciting challenge to her."

Dasan's eyes moved to Erin's necklace, to Avanyu, whose voice was thunder, whose spirit carried those it touched through the waters of change. "Not this time."

* * * * *

The silence between Kieran and Lyric lasted until he had her inside his house and sitting in a recliner. "You know there are about half a dozen federal agencies looking for the AFF," he growled, placing both hands on the armrest of her chair and leaning over, caging her in.

"Yeah, I know. And I can't tell them a thing. The AFF made sure of that."

The muscle in his cheek twitched. "This goes beyond breaking the rules, Lyric, this moves into fucking crazy territory."

Lyric could feel her temper start to heat up. She was willing to let him vent, to feel a twinge of guilt for upsetting Erin and straying farther over the line than she'd ever been before—but she wasn't crazy, she hadn't jumped in without looking at the cards she'd drawn and deciding how big a gamble she was willing to take. She'd handled herself, avoided doing anything that she wouldn't stand by. She was a professional, same as he was.

"I knew what I was doing."

She could almost hear him gritting his teeth. "You think Grandma would be happy if you got killed trying to get her dogs back? You think John Merriman or any of those other people expected you to risk your life in order to get their dogs back?"

"I didn't do it for them. I did it because I thought it needed to be done."

"And you fucking got shot!"

"And that doesn't happen to cops? You've never been in a tight spot when you were undercover or working a case?"

His knuckles went white against the dark fabric of the recliner. "Don't even go there, Lyric. There's a big difference between what I am and what you are."

Icy shards of pain threatened to shatter in Lyric's heart. As quickly as her anger had started to rise, hot and volatile, it dissipated against the cold barrier of self-protection. "And that difference is what, Kieran?"

The tone of her voice, the look in her eye, the subtle body language were all the warning Kieran got. In the span of a heartbeat his world shifted and changed. Son of a bitch. Here it was. Win, lose, or draw. Cards on the table or she'd walk and take a chunk of his soul with her.

Kieran forced as much of the anger away as he could. Forced enough away so that he could think a little more clearly, put together an answer that would work for both of them. When he had one, he leaned in so that their faces were only inches apart. "You want to know what the difference is between us, Lyric? I don't go in alone when it's dangerous. I always have backup, a partner to share the risk with." He moved in even closer, forehead-to-forehead. "I'm going to let you skate this time. I'm going to give you the benefit of doubt. But next time, baby, you'd better give me a heads-up if it looks like it could be dangerous. None of this lone ranger shit. It'll really piss me off if I have to visit you in jail or at the cemetery."

He tilted his head and brushed his lips against hers as his hand smoothed along her uninjured side, moving upward and slipping under her bra so that he could cup her breast. "Promise me you won't tangle with the AFF again."

"I'm still going to try and get the dogs."

"No more letting them take you off somewhere without telling me. Christ, Lyric, I'd go crazy if something happened and you just disappeared."

She placed her hand over his heart and felt its reassuring, steady beat. "I can promise that. From now on, you're my backup." She cocked her head. "But it works two ways, Kieran. No more threatening to have me hauled down to jail when I want to work a stakeout."

Goddamn. That'd come back to bite his ass. If she'd been with him…

"Deal." He took her mouth with his, twining his tongue with hers, stroking and teasing so that she had to clamp her legs together to lessen the ache between them. When he pulled away, she said, "That stuff Dasan put on me is still working. I can't feel my injured side at all. If I got on top…"

Kieran's cock throbbed at the suggestion. He stood, helping her to her feet, suddenly needing to bury himself in her hot, slick folds as much as he needed to breathe.

Hours later Kieran was still lodged in her warmth, surrounded by the wet heat of their shared orgasm, as she slept on his chest, the weight of her a welcome affirmation that she was alive, safe, his.

Tomorrow he'd have to think of a way to get some ballistics tests done without drawing attention to Lyric. He needed to know what they were dealing with here. From everything she'd told him about the AFF, there was a reason they'd left the baggie and he didn't think it was an act of goodwill so that Lyric would know her DNA wasn't making its way to the Feds.

He was kind of surprised the Feds hadn't already come knocking on his door. But maybe they hadn't finished processing Leila's house and the sale site.

Son of bitch. Kieran was honest enough to admit to himself that he didn't want to close his eyes and see the sights Lyric had described—not the least of which was the military precision and intel capabilities of the AFF. Fuck, he'd rather go against organized crime any day.

He was still awake and pinned underneath Lyric when the phone rang. She jerked out of her sleep and gasped. He eased her onto her good side and scrambled for the phone, his eyes immediately finding the clock. Shit. Nobody called with good news at five in the morning.

Chapter Sixteen

"Hey, Kieran, this is Cady. You and Lyric might want to get over here."

"What's wrong?"

"Nothing. John Merriman's dog is here. Erin's already called him, she's on her way to meet him at the emergency vet clinic right now. We think the other two belong to your grandmother. Someone put them in Lyric's backyard and they started barking. Erin heard them first, she called me, but neither of us saw anyone leaving."

"We're on our way."

Kieran hung up the phone. Christ, he couldn't deny the joy that was whipping through him. He speared his fingers through Lyric's hair and pulled her face to his, giving her a quick hard kiss before saying, "Looks like your new acquaintances have given up at least three of the dogs. That was Cady. Merriman's dog and two others got dropped in your backyard."

Lyric's heart raced at the news. She scrambled off the bed and got dressed, stopping only long enough to put some more of Dasan's salve on her side. Already she thought it looked better.

Before they made it out of the house, Kieran's grandmother called. "I want to go with you," she demanded before he could begin giving her reasons not to.

"Lyric and I are leaving right now," Kieran said without thinking.

"Lyric's with you?"

Kieran could practically hear the wedding bells and see the ceremony that his grandmother was envisioning. "Yeah, she's here. We'll be over in a few minutes." He felt compelled to warn her, "They're probably your dogs, Grandma, but try not to get your hopes up, okay?"

His grandmother chuckled. "You're such a good grandson, Kieran. You've always worried and fussed and made me feel loved."

Kieran shifted uncomfortably. Christ. He needed to get back to work before he got a reputation for being a sensitive guy. "We're on our way, Grandma, see you soon." He hung up and shot Lyric a warning glance in case she felt compelled to say anything. She smiled and turned away.

* * * * *

Anna cried when the dogs greeted her at Cady's door. Kieran shifted from foot to foot and looked at Lyric, silently demanding that she do something as his grandmother's tears continued even though her two dogs did their best to lick them off her face. Instead of hugging his grandmother, Lyric moved over and wrapped her arms around his waist. "Chill, baby," she teased. "You can tough this out."

He buried his face against the side of her neck and gave a low growl as he pressed kisses along her smooth skin. Damn if she didn't know exactly how to handle him.

"Any word yet from John or Erin?" Lyric asked Cady.

"Erin called a minute ago. Emily's got a pretty bad viral infection with complications. They've got her on IV fluids with heavy-duty antibiotics to fight secondary infections and pneumonia. That's the bad news. The good news is that they're pretty sure she'll pull through. It's just going to take some time. They want her to stay at the clinic."

Lyric bit down on her bottom lip, not sure what John's financial situation was. "That's going to be expensive."

Cady took a minute to scowl at Lyric. "Erin told me what you did, we can talk about *that* later. In the meantime, we already started planning on raising some money for vet care and boarding and whatever else is needed if the AFF hands off the dogs to you. Some of it can go to help Emily. We figured we could hold a casino night. You've got those friends with the roulette operation, Tyler could run a Liar's Dice table and the rest of us could each man a poker table with the house getting a cut of the action."

Kieran closed his eyes momentarily. Being involved with the Montgomerys was going to mean navigating some dangerous waters. It was probably a miracle that most of Lyric's family hadn't landed in jail at one time of another.

"Maybe you ladies shouldn't discuss this in front of a vice cop," he said.

Cady's eyes widened and he knew that she'd forgotten what he did when he wasn't looking for his grandmother's missing dogs. The little hellion only laughed. "We'll make sure to invite plenty of defense lawyers to the game. Maybe even a couple of judges for good measure."

Kieran only barely managed to keep from smiling. Wouldn't that make for a great headline? *Prominent attorneys and judges rounded up in vice raid.*

Damn she made life interesting. But he didn't dare let Lyric know he thought it was funny. She didn't need any encouragement to break the law.

His humor lasted until the phone call came in from Cash. "You see the morning paper?" his partner asked.

"No."

"We need to talk, Kieran. Soon. Dasan told me about the raid."

Kieran tensed. Fuck. He should have called Cash himself.

"Three of the dogs ended up in Lyric's backyard. We're at her sister's place right now."

"When are you going to be back home?"

Kieran looked at his grandmother. She'd stopped crying and had risen to her feet, no longer clutching the dogs like they might disappear again. "I can drop my grandmother off and be there in thirty."

"Lyric going to be with you?"

"Yeah, she's in on this. Completely in on it."

"Yeah, she's in deeper than you know."

Kieran frowned at the tense edge in Cash's voice. "What's in the newspaper?"

"A long exposé about stolen and giveaway pets and what becomes of them—including photographs of Leila and Tony's yard, complete with dachshunds that we *didn't* see but sans the AFF graffiti and trashing that we *did* see. Oh and there's a nice quote from Lyric."

"Son of a bitch. It's a setup."

"Yeah. That's what I thought. The question is, what's the AFF after now?"

"Shit."

"I'll put in a call to Dasan."

"We'll take Grandma home then head to my place."

"Okay. I'm going to stop by my apartment long enough to shower and change and see if the fish are still alive, then I'll be there. Man, I'll be glad when this is over and you're back. I hate working with Bailey. I just spent eight hours on a prostitute sting with him."

Kieran snorted. Nobody in the department liked working with Bailey. The guy didn't know his ass from a sewer hole. "See you in a few."

"Okay."

"What's going on?" Lyric asked as soon as Kieran pocketed his cell phone.

"Damned if I know. Cash and Dasan are meeting up with us at my place." He leaned over and swooped up one of the dachshunds. Lyric copied his move and got the other one, handing it off to Anna when Anna opened her arms.

Cady grabbed Lyric's arm and pulled her into a hug. "Be careful. And call me if there's something I need to know. I'm on the run doing portraits all day, then Erin and I are supposed to meet up and go riding, but I'll keep the cell phone with me."

* * * * *

Lyric studied Kieran's partner and hid a smile. Oh yeah, she knew his type well enough. He was like her cousin Shane, whose favorite philosophy was "life's a party and I go where my dick leads, but no strings, no attachments, I'm here for the fuck and then I'm moving on".

"Got any ideas what the AFF is playing at?" Cash asked after he'd spread the newspaper on the coffee table in Kieran's TV room.

Kieran and Lyric both leaned over to read the article. She frowned when she saw the quote attributed to her. *In a recent interview, Lyric Montgomery, a local detective specializing in animal-related cases, indicated that she's seen an alarming increase in the number of dachshunds, like those pictured below, disappearing in both California and Nevada. She suspects that the animals are being collected and "bunched" by someone intending to sell the dogs to an organization that will subject them to experimentation.*

Edginess hummed down Lyric's spine, especially when she saw that her cell number was included at the end of the article. There were some rescue numbers and shelter numbers, to make it appear as though her number wasn't singled out for inclusion. But she knew that was an illusion. Lyric looked again at the byline. Not only hadn't she spoken to anyone named Eric Helquist, but she didn't recognize the name.

"There's no mention of the AFF," Kieran said, putting his hand on the back of Lyric's neck and gently messaging her tense muscles.

Cash shifted in his chair. "No mention of the raid on the sale, either." He grimaced. "Speaking of which, a Fed caught me on the way out. Special Agent Lucero. Wanted to know how it was we stumbled on the AFF operation at Price's house."

Fear rolled through Kieran's gut. "You think Lucero is going to come looking for Lyric?"

Cash shook his head. "I doubt it. But who knows with the Feds. They're too good to share information with the locals."

Dasan tapped the newspaper. "Anyone call the newspaper and talk to the guy who wrote this?"

Kieran shifted in his seat. "I'll do it."

Lyric stopped him with a hand on his arm. "I'll do it. If you call as a cop, he's just going to cite the First Amendment and clam up about his sources. But if I call, especially as a quoted source, I'll have his balls in a vise."

All three men grimaced at the imagery. Then Cash grinned at Kieran. "I'm glad she's with you, partner."

Kieran leaned over and brushed his lips over Lyric's. "Me too. Go for it."

Lyric made the call but got passed to voice mail. She didn't recognize the voice, but she left a message and said she expected a call back.

They hashed over possible AFF objectives through another pot of coffee before Dasan had to break off to go collect a skip. "This loser is on the clock when it comes to sex," the bounty hunter said as he stood up. "Same time, same place, same girl, same position every time. The guy's usual hooker turned him in for a quick hundred. I was planning on collecting him before he banged her, but she didn't want to be cheated out of the money. Says he'll be done five minutes after she takes him in the room."

Kieran and Cash both snickered. Lyric rolled her eyes.

"He local?" Kieran asked.

"No. Skipped bail in Vegas. Soon as I grab him, I'm heading there. I've got some more work waiting. As soon as it's wrapped, I'm moving my operation here. But if something breaks and you guys need me, call."

"I thought you hated it here, except for short stops," Cash said.

Dasan's gaze traveled to the snake that lay stretched out in its habitat. "Things change." He looked at Lyric. "How's the side?"

"Can't feel a thing."

"Okay if I take a look at it?"

Lyric stood and lifted her shirt, surprised by how much more healed the wound seemed since she and Kieran had gotten out of bed only a few hours ago. "Your salve is pure magic."

Dasan gave a small smile and nodded. "It's an ancient recipe. Do you have it with you?"

Lyric pulled the tin from her back pocket and handed it to him. Dasan opened it and coated his finger with the salve. He stroked along the line of stitches and the smell of the desert washed over her while the heat from his fingertip felt like it reached deep into the wound.

When he was finished, Dasan handed the tin back to Lyric. "You won't need to use much more of this."

Lyric's sixth sense hummed. Damn. She wished he wasn't leaving. Grandma Maguire would love to meet him.

Dasan looked at Cash and cocked his head toward the door. "Got a second before I head out?"

"Sure."

* * * * *

Cash took his eyes off the road just long enough to look at the dog that was settled on a blanket and lying on the floor in front of the passenger seat. How the hell had he been talked into this? Why weren't Lyric and Kieran making this trip?

He had to immediately shut down his mind after that question. He did *not* want scenes of Kieran and Lyric doing the horizontal monkey to flash through his thoughts. Fuck, being around those two was like being dropped into a furnace.

Shit, he could see why Kieran fell so hard for her. Man…the time he'd seen her with Braden paled against being around her up close and personal. He'd gotten a hard-on just from seeing her flat little belly when she'd lifted her shirt to show Dasan her wound.

Goddamn, if that wasn't pathetic, then Cash didn't know what was. As soon as he got home from this little errand and caught up on some sleep, then he was going to pull out his PDA and hook up with someone, maybe even a couple of someones—like those twins that liked to share everything. Yeah, he could go for some mutual, no strings attached sharing.

Cash looked at the dog again. When they'd found it underneath the garbage yesterday, he'd thought it was a goner. It still didn't look too good, but the vet's office had called and said it could go home. They'd even scanned it and found out where home was—an hour and a half away with a couple of old people who were afraid to drive on the freeway.

Cash worked his shoulders, trying to loosen some of the tension. When Kieran had come out to tell them about the dog making it, Dasan had pulled his shaman shit, going all mystic and insisting Cash had to be the one to make this trip—that he'd seen it in a fucking dream.

Cash slowed down to start watching for the Ericksons' address. A house halfway down the block was an advertisement for patriotism. American flags everywhere. Army and Marine flags. He got closer and saw the "support our troops" ribbon on the front door just as he noticed the number. It was the Ericksons' place.

The dog—Cash thought Kieran said its name was Rosy—began wagging its tail and struggling to get up. "Hold on, girl." The last thing he wanted was for the dachshund to have some kind of a relapse before he could turn it over to its owners.

An old lady opened the door before Cash had even stopped the car. By the time he'd climbed out and moved to the passenger door, a frail old man in a wheelchair was next to her. Cash's throat tightened. Shit, this was like looking at a portrait of his grandparents before they'd both passed away.

He leaned over, blocking the sight from his eyes but not his mind as he picked up the dog. It was still thumping its tail weakly and now that he was touching it, its body seemed to be vibrating with a single thought. Home.

It shot right to Cash's gut. Fuck. There was a time when he knew what that meant.

"Rosy," the old man croaked as Cash moved up the walkway and the dog whined. Cash got to the couple and saw that the man had a thick towel folded on his lap. Answering Cash's silent question the man patted the towel. "I'll hold her."

Cash lay the dog on the towel, his throat tightening again at the sight of the trembling old hands that immediately began stroking the dog. He dug in his pocket for the antibiotics that the vet had sent, along with the instructions, intent on handing them off and getting the hell back to his apartment.

The old woman took hold of his wrist, her skin looking pale and fragile against his. "You've driven so far.

Please come inside. I just made a batch of sun tea, let me pour you a glass."

Somehow Cash found himself being led into their house, following behind as the woman pushed the wheelchair so that her husband wouldn't have to stop petting Rosy. The sensation of sandpaper rubbing over Cash's flesh increased with each step down the narrow hallway, only to explode into full-fledged panic when he got to the room at the end of the hallway and saw the woman sitting there. She gave him a smile that had his heart hungering for another one and said, "Not enough room for two wheelchairs in the hallway."

Cash's eyes dropped to her cast-bound legs as the old man's chair stopped next to hers and she leaned over to stroke the dog. It all came together for him them. The American flags. The Army and Marine flags. The Support our Troops ribbon. The way she had the tanned, fit look of a soldier.

He studied her while her attention was on the dog. Felt almost unable to take his eyes off of her, like he could spend a lifetime looking at her. Panic clawed at his gut with that realization.

Cash set the antibiotics and the veterinarian's instructions down on the coffee table. "Here are some pills for the dog. The vet said to feel free to call if you have any questions. I've got to head back."

His abruptness startled all three of them. He could read it on their faces when they looked up. Awareness ripped through him when his gaze connected with the woman's. She cocked an eyebrow in challenge. *What's wrong, you scared to be around us?*

Hell yeah. He was scared all the way down to his core.

The elderly woman's hands fluttered in agitation as she patted her pockets. "Taryn, do you remember where I put the money?"

"Silverware drawer, Grandma."

When she moved toward a door leading deeper into the house, Cash said, "You don't owe me anything."

The elderly woman stopped and looked at him uncertainly. "We've offered a reward."

Cash shook his head. "That's not necessary."

The elderly man spoke up. "Take the money. Rosy means more to us than..." His eyes teared and he swallowed hard. "She's more than just a pet. She belonged to our grandson. We promised that we'd take care of her until he came back. Now she's ours. When we lost her..."

Taryn reached over and squeezed her grandfather's hand. "She's back now, Grandpa. TJ'd be really mad if you made yourself sick and had to go to the hospital. You know he would."

Cash's heart squeezed at the pain he saw reflected on their faces. His soul felt battered and torn, his mind confused, pulled between the desire to escape and the unexpected need to stay.

Taryn looked up and their eyes met again. "My brother was killed by a suicide bomber."

"Marine?"

She smiled and it flowed straight to Cash's heart, filling it to the point that it was hard to breathe. "Lucky guess. Yeah. He was a Marine. I'm Army." Her eyes dropped to her cast-encased legs. "Ex-Army now."

A cold fear washed over Cash as his eyes followed hers. His head buzzed with the need to know what happened to her, what *would* happen. His gut churned with possible answers, possible outcomes.

The elderly woman moved again, heading toward the door that probably led to the kitchen. "Please don't," Cash said, stopping her again. "Look, I'm a cop. This is all in the line of duty."

Surprise flickered across the woman's face and she glanced quickly at her granddaughter. Taryn gave a small shake of her head before saying, "We owe you for the veterinary expense. At least let us reimburse you for that."

"No. It was donated." The lie slipped out, but once he told Kieran to forget about reimbursing him, it'd be true.

"Let me get you a glass of tea at least," the elderly woman said.

Cash desperately wanted to say yes, and that alone was enough for the panic to settle in again. With each moment in their presence he felt like he was being sucked into their lives, their world.

"I can't, I really need to head back."

He escaped to his apartment, telling himself that it was just the long hours and lack of sleep that had caused him to overload when he dropped off the dog. But in his dreams a white snake slithered out of the desert, coiling in front of him, its presence blocking his way and urging him to turn around and go back.

Cash woke up cursing. Fuck Dasan and his visions.

Chapter Seventeen

Kieran saw the shape of the AFF plan a few days later. Son of a bitch. They were using the dogs, and therefore Lyric, as bait in order to draw Leila and Tony out into the open.

Fuck. He'd should have seen it before, should have known that the return of Merriman's and his grandmother's dogs was more than just a payoff to keep Lyric from stirring up the shit.

If he hadn't tuned in to the news, he'd still be operating blind. But there it was in Technicolor, a special-interest piece about the anonymous return of some show dachshunds in Reno, along with a quick pan to a woman clutching one of the dogs and saying she'd lost hope until a pet detective out of California contacted her.

Kieran muted the TV and reached for the phone to try and track down Lyric. When he did, he noticed the voice mail waiting on the cell. His guts went cold at the sound of his friend in ballistics' voice. "Hey, this is Carson. Just a heads-up, Kieran. I got an unexpected visit from Special Agent Lucero when I ran the ballistics on that bullet you brought in. The Feds had the file flagged. The same gun was used in a drive-by down in LA. Guy by the name of Leroy Bruttel. I put in a call to a friend of mine down there. Bruttel was in the animal buying, selling, fighting, killing, you-name-it business. If this is about your grandmother's dogs...just be careful, buddy. Like I said, you've got a Fed sniffing around and a drive-by shooter out there."

* * * * *

Lyric had pretty much decided that no one could make cinnamon rolls like John Merriman. She polished off her second roll and licked her fingers as John moved to the refrigerator and cut off another piece of hotdog for Emily.

Three days of IVs and veterinary intervention, along with whatever emergency care that the AFF had provided, had meant the difference between life and death for the red dachshund.

John returned to the table and fed a small sliver of hotdog through the door of Emily's crate. Once she'd started feeling better, they'd discovered that her spine had been injured. The vet wanted her confined for at least a week in the hopes that they could avoid an operation.

Lyric shifted in her seat, wishing that Erin or Cady were here to handle this. They were better at this kind of stuff than she was. She stalled a minute longer by taking a sip of her coffee, then plowed in. "I haven't given up on getting the other dogs back. Altogether there could be over a hundred of them, maybe even twice that. It'll be easy to get the ones with microchips back home. It'll take a while to sort through the others and either find their homes or find them new homes. People involved in rescue work will probably help, but it's going to take some money to cover boarding, veterinary expenses, travel, stuff like that until all the dogs have been taken care of." She shifted again and eyed a cinnamon roll wondering if this would be easier if she ate a third one.

John's hand wavered and she braced herself before adding, "Erin and Cady are already planning a casino night to raise money. We'd like to use some of it to help with Emily's expenses."

Tears formed at the corners of John's eyes and Lyric wanted to crawl under the table. She settled for the third cinnamon roll.

John reached over and patted her free hand with one of his. "You've already given me a gift beyond value, several gifts in fact. I've got enough to comfortably handle Emily's expenses. Send me an invitation when you hold your casino night. I'd like to attend." He gave a shaky laugh. "Let's just hope Anna's grandson doesn't get wind of it and conduct a vice raid. Even retired judges have to worry about their reputations."

"You were a judge?" The now-healed bullet wound on Lyric's side burned with a touch of worry.

"Started out as a lawyer, finished as a judge." At the slightly wary expression on Lyric's face, he added, "I handled family law cases, not criminal ones."

"That's good to hear," Lyric said before being drawn from the conversation by the ringing of her cell phone. She didn't recognize the number, but then she hadn't recognized a lot of the numbers since the article in the newspaper came out.

The sheer volume of calls, many from people who'd lost their dogs or wanted to adopt one of the dogs pictured with the article, gave Lyric hope that the AFF intended to transfer the animals to her.

Lyric answered and a female voice immediately gushed, "Oh, I'm so glad I caught you in. You don't know me, but my name is Livia Thompson and my dachshund was stolen several weeks ago. I'd just about given up all hope of finding Prince again until I saw that article in the newspaper. One of the dogs pictured looks just like Prince. I just know it's him. Where is he now? Can I come over and see him?" She gasped, "Please don't tell me that he's...dead."

The skin along Lyric's body was tingling. "I don't have any dogs here."

The woman on the other end of the phone started crying. "But...but, it said in the paper that you have them. Please, please tell me there's a chance I'll get him back."

Her crying didn't bring a rush of compassion to Lyric, it only caused the warning bells to ring even louder. She'd talked to enough "honest" people to feel the difference between them and this caller. Suspicion moved up her spine along with the humming of her sixth sense.

According to Celine, Leila Price had left small-town America and headed for Hollywood — presumably to be an actress. Well, by all accounts, and if Lyric's hunch about who she was talking to was correct, Leila had succeeded in becoming one.

Lyric decided to test her theory by saying, "I'll need to get your name, telephone number, and address. Then I'll need a description of your dog. If I determine whether or not he was one of the dogs rescued, then I'll contact you."

"If you're not going to let me come over and get Prince right now, then you're going to hear from my lawyer," Livia said in a convincingly belligerent tone before slamming the phone down.

Lyric reshuffled her thoughts and came up with a different game than the one she'd been lulled into thinking that the AFF was playing. When Kieran called a few minutes later and told her about the publicity surrounding the return of the show dogs, she knew they'd both reached the same conclusion. "Looks like it's working. Leila just called. She wanted to come see the dogs. I played along, but as soon as I asked for personal information, she decided to threaten me with a lawyer and hung up."

"You let her think you had the dogs?" The tone of his voice let Lyric know just what he thought of that move.

Lyric glanced at John. "Why don't we talk about this later?"

"Later had better be in about fifteen minutes. Where are you?"

"At John's house."

"I hope I'm hearing the sounds of you standing up and saying goodbye."

Lyric laughed. "Did anyone ever tell you that you're overbearing?"

"You can tell me when you get here—just make sure it happens in less than twenty minutes. See how generous I can be? I'm giving you five extra so you don't have to speed."

Short of calling in the Feds, Kieran couldn't think of a way to put Lyric into protective custody until this thing with the dogs blew over. Raw fear washed over him again as he thought about his friend in ballistics' call. Christ, how the fuck was he going to keep Lyric safe? And what was she thinking about to play along with the AFF's game?

Kieran stopped pacing and stared at the snake. Shit! He knew what she was thinking about. The dogs. She couldn't let it go.

Hell, he wasn't completely happy with the outcome, either—he'd stood in Rickard's and then Price's backyard and seen how the dogs had been kept. He still had fucking nightmares about what Lyric had seen at the sale. But years of being a vice cop had taught him to work each case until it was done and move on, to compartmentalize as best he could and figure that when hunting scum, there was always going to be another chance to take them down.

Goddammit. This case was closed. His grandmother had her dogs. Merriman had his dog. And they'd even scored a bonus and gotten a fifth dog.

Thinking about that dog put a scowl on Kieran's face. Christ, if he'd known driving the dog to its owners was going to put Cash on a short fuse, he'd have held off making love to Lyric long enough to take the drive himself! Fuck. For the last three days his partner was surly enough to make even the horniest ladies at the station avoid him.

Kieran moved to the front of the house. A car pulled up in the driveway and he angled over to the window, making sure it was Lyric before checking his watch. Eighteen minutes. He'd half-expected, hell, he'd half-anticipated that she'd be late just to stir him up. He opened the door for her. The little hellion stopped in front of him and gave him a smile that said she knew what he'd been thinking.

Her gaze lowered and roamed over his body. Kieran's cock pressed even harder against the front of his jeans. Damn if the thing hadn't developed a mind of its own and the only thing on it was Lyric. She licked her lips and it…he…wanted to rip open the jeans and jump her. Son of a bitch, she was a tricky one, trying to distract him when they needed to talk. He closed the door. If that's the way she wanted it, he'd give it to her, then they'd talk.

"You know I'm not very happy with you, baby."

She laughed and stepped into him, twining her arms around his neck and pressing against him. "What can I do to make you happy?" she whispered before brushing her mouth against his, then sucking his lower lip between hers.

Kieran let her play for a few heartbeats before taking control, sealing their mouths together and demanding entry with his tongue. She rubbed against him and the heat she generated felt like it was going to burn him alive. His hands went to her ass, pressing her tightly against him as his tongue twined and stroked and seduced hers into sucking on it. His cock twitched and jerked, wanting the same attention.

Goddamn, when he was with her he couldn't think of anything but getting her naked and making love with her, of feeling her hands and mouth on him and returning the favor, biting and sucking her breasts before burying his face against her bare cunt and worshipping her until she shuddered and screamed and drenched him with her pleasure.

Kieran pulled away, needing to breathe, needing to get them out of their clothes. "Bed," he growled, stripping out of his shirt as he led her in the direction of his bedroom.

The sight of the freshly healed bullet wound on her side sent a wave of urgency through him, a need both fierce and tender. He'd keep her safe even if he had to get tough with her to do it.

"Get on the bed, baby," he ordered as soon as she was out of her clothes, the throb in his cock escalating at the saucy look she sent his way. Then damned if the little hellion didn't slip backward, spreading her legs so that he could see her glistening, wet slit.

"Like this, Kieran?" her voice was a challenging purr that stroked up his spine. "Is this the way you want me?"

Christ, she almost sent him to his knees with her antics. He joined her on the bed, unable to keep his fingers from smoothing over her bare cunt, teasing around her clit before slipping into heated wetness. "Oh no, baby, that'd be too easy." He gathered her juices and trailed downward, over her virgin back entrance. She tensed and a feral pleasure ripped through him. "I promised we'd get to that, and here we are. Afraid?"

"No."

"Prove it. Get on your hands and knees."

She took her time doing it, dragging it out until his body was coated with a light sheen of sweat. Damn if she didn't know just how to get him worked up. Well, two could play at that.

He opened the drawer of the nightstand and pulled out a tube of lubricant, dropping it on the bed next to them before moving over her and kissing along her spine, her neck, the delicate shell of her ear as he slipped his cock between her thighs, bathing in her wetness, sliding back and forth over her clit, and savoring the feel of bare skin on bare skin.

She whimpered and arched, trying to make him slide inside her cunt, and he brought his hand down in a sharp smack across her buttock. "Oh no, baby, you aren't calling the shots here."

Lyric cried out and tried to entice him to enter her again, sobbing when another stinging smack landed on her ass cheek. Kieran gritted his teeth against the need to shove himself inside of her pussy and start fucking as she pushed the limits, driving them both higher.

When he couldn't hold off any longer he pulled back and reached for the lubricant, ordering her to grab the headboard. She complied and he coated his fingers with the lubricant before leaning over her and teasing her back entrance, slipping his finger in and out, preparing her, reveling in the way her body shivered and shook, in the way she finally pleaded, "Oh god, Kieran, please fuck me. Don't make me wait any longer."

"Fuck you how, baby?" he asked, positioning the head of his cock at her tiny, virgin hole.

"Any way you want to," she whispered.

His penis jerked in response and he pushed into her, into the tight fist of muscles that had never known another man. She sobbed and shook underneath him as he moved deeper.

"Don't fight it, baby, just relax."

She shivered and arched, her cries when he retreated from her body testing Kieran's control. He slipped his hand around to pet her sweet cunt and rub her engorged clit. "Is this okay, baby? Does this feel good?"

"Oh god, Kieran. Please!"

He began pumping then. Moving in and out, riding the thin edge of pleasure and pain with her until they were both shaking, both covered in sweat, both careening toward orgasm, and then his cries of release joined hers.

They moved to the shower then and he soaped her body, kissing away the tears on her face. "You liked it, didn't you?" he whispered against her lips.

Lyric rubbed against him, completely submissive, overwhelmed. God, when had she started needing him like she needed her next breath of air? "Yes."

He hugged her tightly, his thoughts turning to how he was going to keep her safe. "My buddy in ballistics called. He got a hit on the bullet. Looks like Tony used it on a guy named Bruttel in a drive-by shooting. Want to guess what line of work Bruttel was in?"

She shivered and pulled back, taking the soap from him and lathering first her hands and then his body. "I don't need to guess. Bruttel was Leila's sugar daddy. She started out a bed buddy and ended up taking over his business."

"I want you to leave town. Have Bulldog send you out on a case until this thing settles down and the Feds leave."

"I can't, Kieran."

He closed his eyes, frustrated by her answer, but not surprised. He wanted to grab her arms and shake some sense into her — or at least some fear. But...

Christ, how could he expect her to accept the danger that went with a cop's life if he didn't accept what she was, who she was? At least most of Bulldog's cases, hell, most of hers, weren't like this one.

They left the shower and returned to the bedroom. Kieran found his jeans and put them on. "Do you know how to use a gun?"

Lyric laughed. "Sure. The Montgomerys and the Maguires have always fought it out at the gun range."

Kieran paused, shirt in hand. He'd heard someone mention that Braden Maguire was a hell of a shot. "How do the Montgomerys stack up?"

"Individually or when we shoot in teams?"

He leaned over and nibbled along Lyric's neck while one hand moved to cup her still bare breast and tweak the nipple. "How do you stack up, baby?"

Lyric closed her eyes and pushed into his palm, already wanting him again. "When I practice I can beat Braden about half the time. If I don't practice, then both he and Cole can beat me."

"Rifles or pistols?"

She shrugged. "Either."

"What do you have at your house?"

"Neither. Grandpa Maguire has a huge collection. I use his guns if I'm shooting solo. If I'm practicing with Braden or Cole, they bring extras."

Kieran's attention shifted from her breast and neck to the nightstand next to the bed. He opened the drawer and retrieved a gun, along with a holster, and set them on the nightstand. "Until this blows over, I want you to carry this."

She gave a small husky laugh that tightened Kieran's balls. "I don't have a permit to carry a concealed weapon."

"I'll take care of it."

Kieran's lips returned to her neck, then moved up to her ear and she shivered in response, pressing tight against him. Christ, he wanted her again. He sucked the earlobe into his mouth, momentarily forgetting the conversation. Her fingers tucked under the waistband of his jeans and his cock stirred, ready to fill again, anxious to rise and meet her hand. She turned her head so that their lips met. "I love you, Kieran."

His heart expanded, taking up the breadth of his chest and leaving no room for air. Her declaration was like a knockout punch. He hadn't realized how desperately he needed to hear her admit it until the words were out in the open.

He tumbled her backward onto the bed and settled over her, his eyes locking with hers. "I love you, too, baby." He kissed her then, deep and fierce, wanting her to know just how overwhelming what he felt was, how much a part of him she'd become.

When her hands freed his cock, thought turned into action, into the driving need to be one body. Her panties disappeared underneath their combined efforts, and then he slipped home, into wet, silky heat and the feel of her heart beating just as desperately as his was.

Afterward they showered again, lingering to kiss and touch and savor what they had together before reality intruded.

As they got dressed, Lyric's phone rang. She picked it up, smiling when she saw the display. "It's your grandmother."

The smile turned to a frown as she answered the phone and listened to the quiver in Anna's voice as she requested that Lyric come over right away.

"Is something wrong?"

"No." Anna's voice shook before adding, "I need to hang up now."

Kieran's face was tense. "What's going on?"

"I don't know. She wants me to come over right now."

His face tightened. He reached for the shoulder harness and tossed it to Lyric. "You know how to use one?"

She tried to lighten the mood. "Please, you're talking to one of the Fast-draw Montgomerys. Between Grandpa

Maguire's love of guns and Grandpa Montgomery's love of all things gambling related, just about anything that combines the two is a given in our family." She demonstrated by putting on the harness, slipping the gun in its designated place, then drawing.

The worry lines on Kieran's face disappeared for a minute. "Damn, maybe I better talk you into joining the force."

Lyric rolled her eyes. "My self-respect has already taken a serious beating. I'm involved with a cop, for god's sake."

Kieran pulled her to him and pressed a quick kiss to her mouth. "There are compensations."

She rubbed against the front of his jeans. "Yeah, for you, too."

"But I'm not complaining about being involved with a reformed lawbreaker." He held her to him for a long minute, before easing her away. "Let's go see what's going on with Grandma."

* * * * *

"Nice work, Granny," Leila said as Anna hung up from calling Lyric. "Now you had better scrounge up some crates and put the dogs in them before my friend gets trigger-happy."

Tony's lips quirked up at the corners in a parody of a smile. His pale blue eyes were emotionless. The sight chilled Anna even though she already knew that he was a monster with no soul. He and Leila both were.

Her heart cried out at the sight of John's bruised face. She'd refused to call Lyric at first, but when Leila had whipped her pistol across John's face, and then Tony had added punches and kicks, not stopping even when John had fallen to the floor, Anna couldn't bear it. Now she prayed that Lyric was with Kieran, that somehow they'd guess…

"I said get the dogs put in crates," Leila ordered and Tony's lips widened as he pointed the gun at John. John didn't make a sound, though Anna knew his fear and heartbreak had to be as great as her own.

"I've got two travel carriers in the pantry," Anna said, barely recognizing the thin thread of her own voice.

Tony motioned with the gun. Anna moved to the pantry with Tony behind her.

"Not you, old man. Sit down in one of those chairs and put your hands behind you," Leila said when John would have followed.

* * * * *

Kieran frowned at the sight of the flat tire. He knelt down and saw the nail. Fuck! Where had that come from?

"We can take my car," Lyric said.

That was what he was trying to avoid. Having Lyric's car anywhere near his grandmother's house. He stood, weighing his options. Anything besides taking Lyric's car would delay them. He held out his hand for her keys. "I'm driving." She laughed and his mood lightened.

They were a block away from Anna's house when Lyric's cell phone rang. As soon as she answered it, a man said, "Do you recognize my voice?"

Lyric's heart rabbited in her chest. Oh yeah. She recognized it all right. Her eyes cut over to Kieran. "Yeah, I was the guest of honor at a meeting you chaired. You even sent a Caddy to pick me up, complete with literature and black mask."

Kieran braked and pulled over. His frown was enough to blister Lyric's soul.

"I can't talk long," Lyric said.

"Neither can I before I have to dispose of this phone." The man laughed. "I'm surprised you'd choose a cop for a boyfriend."

She stilled, nerves clawing at her insides as they had before. "You've got someone following me."

"Watchers are important when you're being hunted like we are. More so now that Agent Lucero has arrived on the scene."

Lyric was momentarily distracted by the mention of the federal agent. She looked at Kieran and could see the desire to rip the phone out of her hands escalating by the second. This might be her last contact with the AFF. "You said that you'd turn the dachshunds over to me."

"Agreed. That's the purpose of this call. The cell voted to release the dogs to you. Unfortunately they're being housed in a rough neighborhood. We thought it only fair to provide you with a means of protecting yourself when you went to get them. So we took the liberty of putting a gun under your driver's seat. It's loaded, but then the Montgomerys and Maguires are all comfortable around guns. Someone will be in touch with the location. And just a friendly warning, our sources say that your phone lines are secure now, but I wouldn't trust them to stay that way much longer." The call dropped. Lyric slipped her phone back into her jacket pocket.

"That was them," Kieran said, his grip tightening on the steering wheel even though they were stopped.

"Yeah, he said they're going to give me the dogs." A long second passed before she added, "He also said they put a loaded gun underneath my front seat."

The muscle twitched in Kieran's cheek. He retrieved a handkerchief and used it to fish under her seat. A muttered "Goddammit" was confirmation that he'd found it.

His face was tense when he straightened, leaving the gun where he'd found it. "They've been following you?"

"He said they've got watchers. He knew that Lucero was on the scene now."

Kieran's face grew harsher. "They made sure we took your car and then they called before we got to Grandma's house."

Cold fear ripped through Lyric. With a certainty that terrified her, her sixth sense hummed to life. "Are you going to call it in?"

"And have it turn into a hostage situation?" He opened the door. "No. I'm going in. They won't expect anyone to come through the kitchen."

Lyric grabbed his arm and threw his own words back at him. "You know it'll really piss me off if I have to visit you at the cemetery. I'm not going for this lone ranger shit. What happened to 'I don't go in alone when it's dangerous. I always have backup'? They're expecting me to show up, Kieran, don't try and shut me out. Not now. Not when this is my fault. I can handle myself. I can handle a gun. I can handle this."

Christ, he didn't want to risk losing her. If anything happened to her…

His guts churned and his heart froze at the thought of her being in the same room as Leila and Tony. But he read the determination in her face, the confidence, and he knew she was right. If both Leila and Tony had guns, he might not be able to take them both and keep his grandmother safe at the same time.

Kieran leaned over and pressed a hard kiss against her lips. "Give me a few minutes to get in position before you drive off. I love you, baby. Don't mess around. If you have to shoot, go for the kill shot."

Lyric could read the terror on Anna's face the minute the front door opened. She braced herself and watched as Leila stepped into view, a gun held easily in her hand. "Isn't that sweet. Granny calls and you come running." She used the gun to motion for Lyric to step inside and close the door. "You've got our property, and we want it back." She cocked her head in the direction of the kitchen and Tony stepped into view. The picture Tyler had drawn didn't do him justice. Lyric's creep-meter went off the scale when she took in the pale skin and hair and the dead eyes.

"Where's John?" Lyric asked, bracing herself against the worst. His car was parked next to Anna's, and now both Tony and Leila were in the front room.

Leila smiled. "How touching, you're concerned for the old guy, too. Right now he's duct-taped to a chair in the kitchen. Tony would be happy to put a bullet in him if you need proof that we're very serious about getting our property back."

"Not necessary," Lyric said, mind racing, wondering how close Kieran was. Nodding toward Anna, she said, "Why don't you leave her here. There's no point in having to watch two of us."

Leila laughed. "Nice try, but no, I'm not too worried. We've got more than enough bullets to manage the situation. First you're going to tell me where the dogs are, then you're going to show me. And while you're driving, you're going to tell me how you got them away from the AFF. That should make for an interesting story—or maybe you're part of their little group. In that case, it'll be interesting to find out who the other members are." She stroked a finger along the trigger of her gun. "There are quite a few of us who have scores to settle with them."

Lyric thought she heard a sound coming from the back of the house and readied herself. A second later Kieran moved into view, gun drawn, and ordered Tony and Leila to drop their weapons.

They didn't.

There was no time to do anything but react.

Tony's gun shifted immediately to Kieran, but before Tony could pull the trigger, he was falling backward, blood covering his chest.

In the same instant, Lyric fired and Leila dropped to the floor, gun still pointed at Anna, eyes unseeing, the hole in her forehead darkening and filling with blood as the echo from the guns bounced against the picture covered walls.

Kieran knelt down next to Tony and checked for a pulse, then moved on to Leila, just to be sure. No miracles for either of them, and he wasn't upset by that. He stood. "Nice shooting. Now put the gun down before the uniforms get here. I don't want some rookie getting overexcited."

Lyric set the gun down on the coffee table and hugged Anna. "You okay?"

Anna let out a shaky breath and started crying. "I didn't know what to do when they told me to call you. I didn't want to, but then they hit John and..." She gulped and glanced in the direction of the kitchen.

Kieran moved in and joined Lyric, hugged both her and his grandmother, rejoicing in having them both safe. "John's okay," he said against the top of his grandmother's head. "I cut the tape and told him to get out of here and call 911."

Anna pulled out of the hug and wiped tears away. "I'd better open the front door, so the police will know it's safe to come inside."

Kieran frowned. "Where are the dogs?"

Anna started shaking in delayed reaction. "They were going to take them again. They made us put them in crates, and then he...Tony...took them outside. I need to go get them."

Kieran frowned. "He must have moved their car. John's car is the only one that's parked close. We'll start looking for them as soon as the uniforms get here and someone takes charge of the scene." He ushered his grandmother to the front door and opened it to the sound of multiple sirens heading their way.

Lyric's cell phone rang. She almost laughed when she saw the ID. Celine. Was she supposed to believe it was a coincidence?

"Good news," Celine said. "I just got word from my source at the AFF that they've voted to let you have the dachshunds they've got in their sanctuary. They're moving them now, when I get the address, I'll forward it you. My source is also sending me some pictures of a raid they conducted—a sale down in Salinas. The story should hit in a couple of weeks. Well, I've got to run. My boss has me working on a fundraising scandal."

Lyric pocketed the cell phone, her gaze moving to the bodies on the floor of Anna's living room. Was it wrong to kill a killer? To hustle a hustler? To steal from a thief?

She didn't bother trying to work up any guilt. Her gaze found Kieran and he moved to join her, slipping his arms around her and pulling her tight against the hard strength of his body. "Who was that?"

"You don't want to know."

He nipped the side of her neck. "Don't make me get rough with you, baby."

She shivered, feeling the primal need to get naked and mate in the aftermath of surviving a brush with death. "It was confirmation that they're going to let me have the dogs."

His teeth grazed her neck again. "After that happens, then it's done, Lyric. Case closed. Permanently."

When she didn't answer right away he tightened his grip, for some reason making her think of the boa she'd settled into his TV room, but on the heels of that thought was the knowledge that she wasn't afraid that Kieran would suffocate her. She squeezed him back. "Yeah. Case closed. Permanently. We did all right working together. Didn't we?"

"Better than all right." He kissed her, long and slow and full of promise. "We make good partners, baby, the kind that live together, grow old together, and watch each other's backs for a lifetime."

Kix laughed softly at the challenge she'd just issued. He couldn't wait to get her underneath him. Hell, he couldn't wait to get her on top of him. He'd give her a no-holds-barred ride that she wouldn't get anywhere else. Damn, but she was driving him crazy.

Truth be told, he hardly had to lift a finger and the women came running. Between being the sheriff and being part of the Branaman clan, he almost had to use the nightstick to beat them off.

There'd been a couple of fillies along the way who'd tried to play hard-to-get, but Cady was the real deal—a heap of honesty laced together with sensuality. She'd probably be a hellcat in bed—with the right man. And he was planning to be that man.

Kix grinned. She felt the attraction, he'd bet his favorite truck [...]. And her nipples—they'd been as hard as his cock from the moment Adrienne had introduced them. Now he just had to get her to stop dancing out of reach and accept what was going to happen between them.

"Not a bad lead, darlin'. The Weasel sounds like a good man to talk to," Kix said when they were on their way to the racetrack. He couldn't resist the temptation to lean closer and brush the wild curls back from her face.

For a split second she allowed the touch, then color rushed to her face and she jerked away from him. "Do you think you could stay on your side of the truck?"

"I reckon I can try if you really want me to."

Cady risked a glance in his direction and immediately wished she hadn't. He was just...too masculine...too sexy...too adorable...too everything...and definitely too much for her. "Are you sure you're really a sheriff?"

"Yeah, been one for the last five years." He grinned and she was immediately entranced by the sparkle in his eyes and the little dimple next to those kissable lips. His eyebrows moved up and down. "You want me to bring out the handcuffs, or do you want to move right to the nightstick?"

Cady forced her eyes back to the road though she had a harder time forcing erotic images of being cuffed to the bed out of her mind — not that she'd ever even come *close* to experiencing that fantasy, but with Kix — whoa, *nix* that. She was *not* going to get involved with him. He was trouble with a capital H for heartbreak.

When they got to Bay Downs, Cady pulled out her camera and made sure she had release forms along with film. Besides being a great cover for investigating, she genuinely loved photography — it was one of many things she had in common with Erin and Lyric.

Kix quirked an eyebrow. "No digital camera?"

"Not on Bulldog's cases. He wants to have negatives."

Kix picked up her camera case and studied the laminated business card glued to the front. "Cady Montgomery, Professional Pet Photography." He grinned. "This for real?"

"Yes." Cady cringed inwardly when she heard the defensiveness in her voice.

"Would have pegged you for a doer instead of a looker."

"What does that mean?"

A slow grin settled on Kix's face. Damn if she wasn't as prickly as a hedgehog. "I'm just surprised you're a picture taker. Way I've always seen it, there are two kinds of people — those that stand around watching life go by and those that take it by the horns and ride it for all it's worth."

Cady frowned at him. "A person *can* be a professional photographer and live life to the fullest, just like a person *can* be good at multiple things. Not everyone"—her eyes conveyed a silent *like you*—"is good at only one thing. I'm also a good PI and a damn fine poker player."

His laugh stroked right over her. "Well darlin', I'm good at a lot of things, too. In fact, I've been known to play a mean game of strip poker, myself. Maybe later we can see who's better—just to set the record straight."

Before she could stop herself, Cady's eyes dropped to the still very noticeable bulge in his jeans. "Pass."

Kix chuckled. "Darlin', at least hesitate for a minute before you slam my ego."

Her eyes moved back up his body until she met his gaze. God, he was hard to resist. She was a sucker for men who had a sense of humor and didn't take themselves so seriously. "I'll bet you weren't even raised on a ranch. You probably grew up in the city watching westerns."

Kix slapped his hand on his chest. "Darlin', you wound me. I was born and raised on the Kicking A Ranch—home of fine horses, fine cattle and mighty fine men."

"Of which you're the exception."

About the author:

Jory has been writing since childhood and has never outgrown being a daydreamer. When she's not hunched over her computer, lost in the muse and conjuring up new heroes and heroines, she can usually be found reading, riding her horses, or hiking with her dogs.

Jory welcomes mail from readers. You can write to her c/o Ellora's Cave Publishing at 1056 Home Avenue, Akron OH 44310-3502.

Why an electronic book?

We live in the Information Age—an exciting time in the history of human civilization in which technology rules supreme and continues to progress in leaps and bounds every minute of every hour of every day. For a multitude of reasons, more and more avid literary fans are opting to purchase e-books instead of paperbacks. The question to those not yet initiated to the world of electronic reading is simply: *why?*

1. *Price.* An electronic title at Ellora's Cave Publishing and Cerridwen Press runs anywhere from 40-75% less than the cover price of the <u>exact same title</u> in paperback format. Why? Cold mathematics. It is less expensive to publish an e-book than it is to publish a paperback, so the savings are passed along to the consumer.

2. *Space.* Running out of room to house your paperback books? That is one worry you will never have with electronic novels. For a low one-time cost, you can purchase a handheld computer designed specifically for e-reading purposes. Many e-readers are larger than the average handheld, giving you plenty of screen room. Better yet, hundreds of titles can be stored within your new library—a single microchip. (Please note that Ellora's Cave and Cerridwen Press does not endorse any specific brands. You can check our website at www.ellorascave.com or

www.cerridwenpress.com for customer recommendations we make available to new consumers.)

3. *Mobility*. Because your new library now consists of only a microchip, your entire cache of books can be taken with you wherever you go.

4. *Personal preferences are accounted for*. Are the words you are currently reading too small? Too large? Too...**ANNOYING**? Paperback books cannot be modified according to personal preferences, but e-books can.

5. *Instant gratification*. Is it the middle of the night and all the bookstores are closed? Are you tired of waiting days—sometimes weeks—for online and offline bookstores to ship the novels you bought? Ellora's Cave Publishing sells instantaneous downloads 24 hours a day, 7 days a week, 365 days a year. Our e-book delivery system is 100% automated, meaning your order is filled as soon as you pay for it.

Those are a few of the top reasons why electronic novels are displacing paperbacks for many an avid reader. As always, Ellora's Cave and Cerridwen Press welcomes your questions and comments. We invite you to email us at service@ellorascave.com, service@cerridwenpress.com or write to us directly at: 1056 Home Ave. Akron OH 44310-3502.

Discover for yourself why readers can't get enough of the multiple award-winning publisher Ellora's Cave. Whether you prefer e-books or paperbacks, be sure to visit EC on the web at www.ellorascave.com for an erotic reading experience that will leave you breathless.

www.ellorascave.com